Happy Pilgrims

Happy Pilgrims

stories by Stephen Finucan

INSOMNIAC PRESS

Edited by Kate Harding.
Copy edited by Samarra Hyde.
Designed by Mike O'Connor.

Canadian Cataloguing in Publication Data

Finucan, Stephen, 1968-
  Happy pilgrims

ISBN 1-895837-59-6

I. Title.

PS8561.I57H36 2000   C813'.6   C00-930473-8
PR9199.3.F533H36 2000

Some of the short stories in this collection have appeared in periodicals prior to the publication of this collection: "On Angel's Wings" appeared in *Saturday Night* and an earlier version appeared in *Wascana Review*; "A Talk" in *B&A*; "Higher Powers" as 'The Fortune Teller' in *McGill Street*; "The Whispering Lady" in *The Sewanee Review*; "The Honeymooners" appeared in *Dandelion*; "Pineapples and Alaska" appeared in *Queen's Quarterly*; "Could Be Rainin'" appeared as 'A Father's Tale' in *McGill Street*; "Windows" appeared in *This Magazine*.

The publisher gratefully acknowledges the support of the Canada Council, the Ontario Arts Council and Department of Canadian Heritage through the Book Publishing Industry Development Program.

Printed and bound in Canada

The Canada Council | Le Conseil des Arts
FOR THE ARTS | DU CANADA
SINCE 1957 | DEPUIS 1957

ONTARIO ARTS COUNCIL
CONSEIL DES ARTS DE L'ONTARIO

Insomniac Press, 192 Spadina Avenue, Suite 403, Toronto, Ontario, Canada, M5T 2C2
www.insomniacpress.com

ACKNOWLEDGEMENTS

There are many people who offered me kindness and support during the writing of these stories. First and foremost, my family, who supplied me with love and leisure in equal measure. Without their assistance and understanding, this book would not have been possible. I am forever in their debt.

I would also like to thank a number of people who were instrumental in the shaping of many of these stories: Tara Sweeney, for suffering through each of these pieces (and others) in their earliest drafts; Phil Whitaker, for his remarkably astute eye and surefire advice; Paul Saxton, for his sagacity and unfailing friendship; Richard Skinner, for his acumen and bi-continental billiards; Russell Celyn Jones, Andrew Motion, Bruce Jay Friedman and Timothy Findley, for offering the wisdom of their experience; the creative writing students at UEA (1995-6); and Doug Kirkwood, who first encouraged me to take up my pen.

Thanks, too, must go to Kate Harding and Mike O'Connor at Insomniac Press who decided to take a chance on me. Also, thanks to the Canada Council for financial assistance offered during the writing of this book.

This book is lovingly dedicated to my grandparents
Harold and Grace Price.

ON ANGEL'S WINGS

The Orton Founder's Day parade was in full swing and the drunken townsfolk were as happy as foraging pigs. Their shouts and cheers greeted the last float as it made its way around the corner. As every year, the float was sponsored by the Orton Rotary Club and sitting high atop it was the town's fattest Rotarian, Jack McGee, who looked like an enormous toad crammed into his palace guard's uniform. The seams of the costume were stretched beyond their limit and McGee's round, hairy belly protruded from beneath the damp linen shirt. In one hand he held a half-empty whiskey bottle, courtesy of the Reeve; the other he rested on his bloated tummy, thumb firmly planted in his navel.

The crowd was pleased with the foolishly drunk McGee's caricature of the drunken fool, Seamus Ferguson, founder of their small mining town. And to show their approval, halfway through McGee's speech they pelted him with the soft peaches, mouldy plums and spoiled tomatoes they'd been saving for weeks.

Angel Cent did not care for the parade; his mind was on feathers. He sat at the foot of his grandfather's wheelchair and played with the old man's shoelaces while rotten produce sailed through the warm October air. And when the drunks flooded into the street, Angel picked himself up and began to push the chair homeward. He stopped at the steps of the library and looked down at his schoolteacher, Reginald Purvis, who lay there weeping like a baby, an empty rum bottle cradled in his arms. When Purvis saw Angel, he threw himself backward on the steps and cried harder.

By the time Angel and his grandfather reached home, the noise of the celebration had faded in the distance. Angel turned the chair into the back drive and followed it past a drooping willow to the woodshed. He used a piece of firewood to prop the door open and pushed his grandfather inside.

The shed was a simple rectangle of unfinished cedar with a rusted and sagging tin roof. It had a dirt floor with firewood stacked at one end and a sloppily-made workbench at the other. Nails on the walls held broken garden tools and rotting lengths of rope. A pile of mouldy tarpaulins sat in one corner and a number of homemade kites dangled from the rafters.

Angel clicked on the utility light and wedged a broken hoe handle under the wheels of the chair. He looked up at the delicate creations his grandfather had built when his hands and mind had been nimble. Then Angel went to the workbench, pulled a tarpaulin from underneath and dragged it across the floor. Carefully, he unrolled the bundle. It held a large pillow, a roll of chicken wire and a childish pair of papier mâché wings.

The wings had been awkwardly layered with old yellow wallpaper. Angel ran his hand along the leading edge of one wing, then turned his attention to the pillow. He took a small penknife from his pocket and guided the blade through the plastic stitching of the end seam. The pillow opened wide. He arranged the downy feathers according to size, then found a bottle of white glue on the workbench and brought it back to the outstretched tarpaulin. Once he was satisfied with the amount set aside, Angel began pasting the feathers. While he did this, he spoke to his grandfather in a quiet, soothing voice:

"Grandpa, tell me about when I was born."

Angel looked into his grandfather's vacant eyes. The old man used to tell him how the child had not wanted to be born. The mother's labour had been long and tedious. Dr. Crowley had assured them that the baby would not come until morning. Then, in the dead part of the night, a storm raged and the electricity failed. And the child decided it was time to come. After painful hours of pushing and pulling they were able to free him, smeared with blood, from the womb. Spent and triumphant, the mother cried through the darkness to see her son. As the old man, now grandfather, held the screaming child high, the electricity returned and the mother saw her son, illuminated by a bare lightbulb. She wept. He looked like an angel.

"It's a funny name. Isn't it, Grandpa?" Angel said. Then he got up and wiped away the spittle that dangled from the old man's chin.

The parade-goers ran out of steam early and, before the sun had begun to sink, started to stumble out of the Queen's Hotel. Some were collected by their loyal children, while others found the company of fellow drunks. Ultimately, all headed toward their homes. Fat Jack McGee, as usual, was the last to leave. He remained behind in the hotel bar to drain the glasses left behind by his fellow Ortonians. The dregs finished, McGee staggered out of the tavern doors. He wobbled his way down a side street to his pride and joy, a 1973 El Camino, and wedged himself behind the steering wheel. It took him several minutes to find the proper key, but once he did, he happily revved the engine. Then he slipped the car into gear and thundered off down the highway, directly into her path.

Talk of the visitation found its way to the breakfast table. Angel listened as his grandmother recounted the story Madge Downy had told her over the phone earlier that morning. On his way home, Officer Price had seen headlights in the middle of one of Ross Shepard's fields. When he reached the car he found Jack McGee sitting in the open passenger door, his feet on the dead clover, blubbering like a baby. And when McGee saw the policeman, he threw himself on the ground and begged for forgiveness. He mumbled something about not seeing her until it was too late. Price asked who he hadn't seen and McGee rolled over onto his back and wailed: The Mother of God.

"Can you believe that?" Angel's grandmother said, as she plopped porridge into the bowls. "That McGee is such a drunk. He'll do anything for attention."

Any other time Officer Price would have laughed at Jack McGee, as most did, but earlier that day he had stolen a *National Geographic* from Dr. Crowley's office. He'd been reading an article about Lourdes. So when he heard McGee whimpering about The Mother of God, he got frightened. He raced back to his car and drove back to town, returning about a half-hour later with Father Snyde. Back in Shepard's field, priest and policeman combed from roadside to fenceline in search of the injured Virgin.

Angel ate his lumpy porridge while his grandmother droned on. He looked over his bowl at his mother across the table. She was methodically spooning the mush into her mouth, her skin the colour of the porridge-stained milk. Angel tried to meet her eyes but they did not move from her bowl.

Halfway through breakfast, Angel's mother excused herself from the table and rushed to the bathroom. Through the closed door he could hear her retches echo in the toilet bowl. No one acknowledged the sound.

After the toilet flushed, Angel's mother returned to the table, wiping her mouth with the back of her hand. His grandmother collected the bowls and took them to the sink.

"Angel, darling," she said, "it's nice out, why don't you take your granddad for a walk."

Angel was more than happy to dress up the old man and roll him out to the shed. It was cool inside the woodshed, so he tucked his grandfather's hands into his coat pockets before he fetched his bundle from under the workbench.

In the middle of the floor Angel re-stacked the feathers. The wing he'd started the day before was a little more than a quarter finished. Tiny feathers smothered the wallpaper. The completed portion looked full and healthy; it appeared as if the wing was being plucked rather than pasted.

Angel sat hunched over, his face close to the wing. When he reached the halfway point, he stopped and leaned back on his elbows. He looked up into the old man's glassy eyes.

"Grandpa, Mommy's going to have a baby, isn't she?"

He waited, as if to let the question sink in.

"That's what she told Grandma."

Angel waited again. He fiddled with the feathers, spreading them thin, then stacking them high again. He picked up the bare wing and looked closely at its outside edge, then put it down and looked back to his grandfather.

"Is that why you're sick?" he asked, quietly.

The first of the old man's strokes had visited him nine years earlier, when his daughter told him she was pregnant. The attack had been minor and left him with a faint slur. The second left him a vegetable in a chair.

"It's okay if it is," Angel said, as he swept the feathers back into the pillow.

That evening, between midnight and the dead hours of morning, every leaf from every tree in town dropped to the ground.

As she readied him for mass, Angel's grandmother said how strange it was. She had lived in the town more than sixty years and not once had the trees become so totally bare in so short a time. And never so early in October.

She pulled her grandson's collar tight and fastened the button. Then she went to the old man and straightened his tie.

Angel sat at the table while his grandmother sprayed her hair. The door to his mother's room, just off the kitchen, was closed. She had not gone to church with them for the past four Sundays. Although Angel did not wonder why, he wished he could stay home with her. Without calling goodbye, Angel's grandmother collected her husband and grandchild and headed out the door.

The church was uncomfortably warm. Its interior was long and close and the parishioners felt cramped in the pews. High in the rafters, slow turning fans circulated the muggy air.

Angel and his grandmother sat on the far side of the

back pew. The old man, in his wheelchair, sat in the aisle beside them. Angel paid little attention to the ceremony. Normally he would have been content to watch the dust motes float on the pastel rays that broke through the stained glass windows. But it was the lead-lined figures that now held his fancy. His eyes were captivated by the outline of saints' halos, of Jesus and of his mother, Mary. Still, even more than these, Angel was intrigued by the finely detailed wings of the cherubs gathered around the edges of the passions.

On the altar, Father Snyde sped through the service. He delivered the readings from St Paul's Epistles like a barnyard auctioneer. And the Gospel was passed through so quickly the parishioners had trouble following along in their missals.

When Father Snyde started into his sermon he had the immediate attention of all, including Angel. His voice was unusually slow and trembling. His arms were listless in the loose folds of his robes.

"God has revealed himself to us," he said.

People strained forward in their pews. Some had heard but not understood; others had only seen the slight movement of the priest's lips.

"I'm certain that by now news of the wondrous happening in Ross Shepard's field has reached all."

A tide of giggles threatened to wash over the congregation.

"Laugh, my friends," Father Snyde said, in a strangely beneficent voice. "I, too, thought of laughing. For I was there and could see nothing."

"Nothing but a fat drunk," someone whispered in the pew in front of Angel.

When the priest spoke again, his fire had returned.

"But why?" he shouted. His words fell like brimstone from the rafters. "Why must we see to believe? Faith. That is what our Lord tells us we must have. Faith!"

The congregation was confused and nervous. Some could no longer hold their laughter at the thought of the priest stumbling through the clover in the dark.

"But I..."

Father Snyde brought his fists down hard on the dais.

"But I," he wailed, "I did not have faith. Like Moses on Sinai, I needed a sign."

He stopped abruptly. He placed his hands on the edges of the dais and hung his head. The parishioners fidgeted in the pews. The chuckles subsided and the close air returned.

"I awoke this morning, my friends," Father Snyde said, without lifting his head. "I awoke and looked at the trees."

He stared at his flock.

"I have my sign."

The offertory was unusually large. Father Snyde happily counted the money, then went to the vault in his stuffy little rectory office. There he combined that Sunday's collection with what remained of the previous Sundays'. With the accumulated funds neatly wrapped in a brown lunch bag, he jumped into his car and drove out to Jack McGee's mobile home. Without so much as a word of haggling, he bought the 1973 El Camino that had run down the Virgin Mary.

For those who did not heed the first sign, Sunday night brought a second. While the town slept — all except Jack McGee, who was celebrating his new fortune with a case of Canadian Mist in a room at the Queen's — a foot of soft, powdery snow fell unheard and unseen.

Monday morning the buses were unable to safely

navigate their routes, and school had to be cancelled. Children throughout the town happily greeted the day.

Father Snyde welcomed the snow as well. He sat himself down behind his wooden desk and telephoned all the important members of the Knights of Columbus. To each he sang the praises of Providence and revealed his wise purchase. The parish of Our Holy Redeemer, he said, would now be on the map. Having spread his good news, the priest put pen to paper and scribbled a hasty note to the bishop in Kingston. Several times he stopped and smiled, proud to be the owner of what was surely destined to be a holy and profitable shrine.

Angel's grandmother bustled about the kitchen. Her routine had been thrown into chaos. She should have already had Angel off to school and been watching her morning TV programs, but the snow had slowed everyone's pace.

"I can't believe the fool gave him money for that car," she said to anyone who would listen. "And our money to boot."

She circled the table, dropping hard flapjacks onto the plates.

"A petition to the bishop," she huffed. "As if we weren't already a laughing stock."

She stopped a moment to get her bearings.

"Angel, honey, help your granddad with his breakfast."

Angel poured syrup onto the old man's pancakes, then added water from his juice glass. He kneaded everything together with his fork until he was left with a fine mush. In between bites from his own plate he would spoon the muddy broth into the old man's mouth, then wipe his chin with his sleeve.

His mother looked sadly from her plate to the

bathroom door. Her face was as pallid as the morning before. She reluctantly forced down a mouthful and shot another glance toward the bathroom.

"Are you sick, Mommy?" Angel asked.

She looked at him as if she'd been caught out doing something illicit.

"No, dear," she said. "Just a little under the weather, is all."

She looked unhappy to Angel. He thought about telling her that it was Mr. Purvis who'd called to say school was cancelled, but decided not to.

"I'm going to take Grandpa out to the shed," he said.

It took Angel more than an hour to clear the path, but when he'd finished, a long stretch of pale-yellow grass lay bare. In the house he trussed the old man like a Christmas turkey, wrapping him in a heavy woollen lumber jacket, a winter shell, two scarves and a thick pair of mittens. Then Angel led him down the path to the shed.

With half the feathers used, the first wing was completed. Angel lay back on the tarpaulin and admired his work. He held it up for his grandfather to see. The old man's expression did not change.

"Grandpa," Angel said, putting the wing down, "do you think it was really her?"

The old man, bound in his winter costume, continued to stare into space. Angel shimmied himself over to the chair and rested his hand on his grandfather's knee.

"It would be good if it was. 'Cause she's like an angel. And they look after people."

He ran his hand along the cuff of the old man's trousers.

"I'm glad she came."

Angel stood up and kissed his grandfather lightly on the forehead, then sat back down in the middle of the floor.

Tuesday broke warm. The previous day's snow had disappeared and was replaced by the sun. Early that morning, while sipping tea in his book-lined study, Dr. Theodore Crowley pondered Father Snyde's hasty petition. In his leather easy chair, the doctor ran his fingers through his drooping moustache, then scratched the inside of his fat, hairless thigh. He leaned his head back and smiled at the rich dreams that danced like sugar plums through his mind. He knew he had to act quickly.

The doctor was at the bank when it opened. Minutes later, cashier's cheque in hand, he was behind the wheel of his Continental heading toward Ross Shepard's farm. The doctor made it clear to the farmer that he had no time to quibble. A quick cup of coffee later, he was back in his car, the proud owner of the field in which the blessed El Camino still rested.

From the farm, Dr. Crowley drove straight to the church rectory. He found the good Father huddled behind his desk, mulling over names for his shrine. He put forth his proposition. What good, he said, was a holy relic without its hallowed ground? There was no nattering. Father Snyde simply poured some of his favourite claret into two coffee mugs and toasted the partnership. The capital shall be fairly split, said the priest, because the Lord provides for all.

She wouldn't be surprised if the leaves were back on the trees by the afternoon, Angel's grandmother had said as she turned the bacon. There were no early morning phone calls to parents, so children had trudged unenthusiastically back to school.

Angel showed little interest in the business of the school day and whiled away his time drawing fat, naked, winged babies. When he tired of that, he drew several pictures of the Virgin Mary lying in fields of forest green clover.

When the final bell rang, Angel packed himself up quickly. On his way out, Reginald Purvis stopped him in the hallway. The man was rake thin. His long angular head was topped with a shock of black hair. His face was gaunt, its only colouring the shadow of a beard. And his eyes were quick and bird-like. He was no longer the weeping drunk from the library steps.

"How's your mother?" Mr. Purvis asked. He placed an awkward hand on Angel's shoulder.

"Fine," Angel replied.

"Good, good," Mr. Purvis said, looking nervously around the corridor. "Not feeling sick or anything, is she?"

"Only in the morning."

Mr. Purvis pulled his hand quickly from Angel's shoulder. He stretched back and took a deep breath in through his nose. Angel could see the thick hair in his nostrils.

"I see," Mr. Purvis said, trying to deepen his voice. "Well, tell her I said hello."

Angel said that he would and started through the doors. On the steps outside he heard Mr. Purvis call after him.

"On second thought, Angel," he shouted. "Don't bother."

When Angel got home his grandfather was waiting at the door in his chair. His grandmother had sat him there while she watched her afternoon TV programs. She'd put on the old man's coat and toque and left him to sweat.

Angel dropped his backpack on the kitchen table and wheeled his grandfather out the door and across the soggy lawn to the shed. The floor inside was soft and the wheels sank slightly. Angel took an extra tarpaulin from the corner and spread it across the sticky floor, then unravelled his own on top. He looked closely at the finished wing and found a number of tiny bare spots. Carefully, he filled the holes with smaller feathers.

Angel watched his grandfather over his work.

"I saw Mr. Purvis today," he said, as he arranged the pile of feathers.

He pulled another handful from the pillow. Before he started back to glueing, he looked up at his grandfather.

"How come Mr. Purvis won't come see my mommy?"

The old man continued to stare.

"Doesn't he like her anymore?"

It didn't seem to bother Angel that his grandfather couldn't talk anymore. He still liked being with him. He did miss the old man's voice, though. It had been loud and gruff and made him laugh. But he never heard that voice anymore. Now his grandfather just sat in his chair and drooled.

Angel lay back on the tarpaulin and looked at the hodgepodge of hanging kites. He missed them too. The old man use to put them together in the attic, and he'd let Angel dab the glue on the joints. They would fly them together at the baseball diamond near the river.

"Grandpa," Angel said, as he blew at the loose kite strings, "is Mr. Purvis my daddy, too?"

The old man sat in his chair, his toque pulled tight over his ears, his zipper snug under his chin. And stared at the floor.

Wednesday and Thursday passed quietly. The skies remained unchanged and nature seemed to have settled. Dr. Crowley began to worry about his investment. Although he was sure Father Snyde had convinced himself and his flock, the doctor felt the need for another sign. The lucrative dreams of pilgrims began to fade. For the first time in years, he found himself praying — for golfball-sized hail, gale-force winds, locusts, anything.

As for Father Snyde, his faith was not as strong as the doctor believed. With the dawn of the third uneventful day, the priest began to question the wisdom of his abrupt communiqué. He did not worry about his congregation. But without another assertion from on high, he knew the bishop would be displeased.

In Angel's house the normal routine had endured. He ate breakfast amid his grandmother's gossip and his mother's nausea. He went to school and dreamt of wings and the Virgin Mary. He came home and wheeled his grandfather out to the woodshed.

Then on Friday evening, Madge Downy, proprietor of the local boarding house, found Reginald Purvis in his room, dangling from a crossbeam. One end of the toaster cord was around the beam, the other around Reginald's neck.

When Dr. Crowley arrived, he and Officer Price cut the teacher down. There was a note, written in red pen, pinned to the young man's shirt. The doctor tore it loose, read it and stuffed it into his pocket.

From the boarding house, Dr. Crowley went directly to the good Father's stuffy little office. His face beamed as he handed the note to the priest. Both agreed that the incident was unfortunate and that it was a tragedy that the young man could not be buried in the church cemetery.

Pleasantries aside, the two men went their opposite

directions. Father Snyde planted himself behind his desk and drafted another urgent letter to the bishop. Dr. Crowley, a new bounce in his step, headed to his office to fill out the paperwork.

The news reached Angel's house at breakfast the following morning. He listened to his grandmother's side of the conversation as he sprinkled brown sugar on his grandfather's porridge.

"Oh my God. That's horrible."

Angel stirred the porridge into a weak gruel.

"There must be a note. Something."

Angel stopped stirring. His grandmother had the receiver pressed tight to her ear and the cord wrapped around her finger. Her early morning energy had dissipated. After she hung up the phone she pulled out a chair and sat down at the table. Angel could not remember the last time she had done this. Her face was drawn, and Angel could see the striking resemblance between mother and daughter.

"Reg Purvis hanged himself."

The words came hollow and dry from her lips. There was a long silence.

"He's dead?" Angel's mother whispered.

She jumped from the table. Her chair fell over backwards. She ran toward the bathroom but began to vomit before she reached the door. The bile dripped through her fingers as she stood dazed in the middle of the room. Then she turned and ran into her bedroom. The door slammed behind her.

Angel's grandmother went to the door and rested her cheek lightly against it.

"Honey?" she whispered, gently. "Honey?"

Angel remained at the table and spooned porridge into the old man. His grandmother came back and sat down. She looked at him and stroked his hair with an unsure hand.

"Angel, dear," she said, in a quiet voice. "Maybe you should take granddad outside for a little while."

The wings were finished. Angel had pasted the last feather in place late Friday afternoon. He took them both from the top of the workbench and set them on the ground, then busied himself with his next task.

He'd brought his backpack from the house and wrapped the length of chicken wire snugly around its middle. He used a screwdriver to bore holes in the base of each wing, then wired them tightly to the backpack.

Angel set the contraption in the centre of the tarpaulin and stared contentedly at his work.

"Mr. Purvis is with Mary now, isn't he, Grandpa?"

Angel did not look at the old man. He kept his eyes on the wings. They rested on a tilt, balanced on their stiff tips. He reached out with his foot and gently tipped them over. Then he got up and walked to the wheelchair. He took his grandfather's hands in his own. They were ivory-white, except where the light-blue veins ran toward his fingers.

"He's lucky," Angel said. "She'll take care of him."

He let go of the old man's hands and went to the wings. Very carefully, he picked them up and slid his arms through the shoulder straps. He twisted his head around to see how they sat. To make sure they were secure, he jiggled up and down.

"Now the new baby's not going to have a daddy, either."

Angel smiled and bounced his shoulders.

"Just like a real angel's."

On Sunday morning Angel's mother was still in her room. The food his grandmother had left by the door was untouched. Angel sat at the table with the old man while his grandmother touched up her hair and makeup. She called once more to her daughter, then collected her husband and grandson and headed off to mass.

It had snowed again, but no one seemed bothered. People reached for their hats and heavy coats as if it were the middle of January.

Angel and his grandmother sat in their usual pew, with the old man in the aisle. They watched as the priest made a mad dash through the readings and Gospel. When he began his sermon there was none of the previous Sunday's timidity. The man's fervour made the congregation uneasy. His body seemed to wind itself tight beneath his shapeless robe.

"Do you need more signs, people?" His voice reeked with triumph. "Are you yet unbelievers?"

Some people shifted in their pews.

"Do you require that God perform more tricks for your amusement? Is that the price of your faith?"

Others cleared their throats.

"The leaves," Father Snyde continued. "The snow. The sun. The snow again. Maybe this will satisfy you."

The priest shot his spindly arm into the air. In his fist he clutched a crumpled sheet of paper.

"God has spoken again," he shouted. "Through the hands of a sinner."

Angel's grandmother put her arm around him and pulled him close.

"He had faith. A desperate sinner who could not face the shame of his own life. But he had faith," Father Snyde's voice thundered from the pulpit. "Reginald William Purvis believed in our Blessed Virgin."

The priest laid the paper down and slowly smoothed

it. He executed a perfect pause. The congregation was silent. When he spoke again, his voice had the slow resonance of an accomplished actor.

"I hope she will forgive me," Father Snyde read.

A low murmur shuddered through the church.

"My friends. If a sinner can believe…"

Angel's grandmother tightened her grip on him. She nestled him to her bosom.

"Bastard," she muttered.

Outside the church Angel's grandmother stopped to talk to the group of women huddled on the steps. They offered theories as to why the attractive young schoolteacher had strung himself from the rafters. Each was confident of her opinion. When they asked Angel's grandmother what she thought, she smiled and said she wouldn't know.

The door to his mother's room was open when they got home. They found her sprawled on the bathroom floor, the rug beneath her dark with blood. His grandmother threw herself on the floor beside her daughter.

"God, no," she sobbed, holding her daughter's limp body and stroking the damp front of her nightgown. "Please, no."

She turned to Angel.

"Go call Dr. Crowley."

Angel stood in the doorway.

"Do it!" she screamed. "His number's by the phone."

Angel found the number on the telephone table and dialled it. The doctor's wife answered. Her voice was sugary sweet.

"Well, I don't think that's possible, Angel."

Her tone calmed him and he waited for her to speak again.

"He's just getting ready to go see Father Snyde. They're talking business, you know."

"Yes," Angel replied.

"So, you see," she continued, "I don't think he'll be able to come over."

Angel's grandmother started out of the bathroom.

"My mommy's bleeding," Angel said, calmly into the receiver.

His grandmother tore the phone from his ear and shoved him aside. She spoke desperately into the receiver.

"For Christ's sake, Judith," she pleaded. "Send him quick. My baby's dying."

Angel sat on the floor where he had fallen and watched his grandmother. Her cheeks looked bruised and her mascara ran in long grey streaks from her eyes. Tears dripped from her chin and landed on the floor by his feet.

Angel picked himself up and walked to the bathroom door. He looked at his mother. She seemed peaceful, as if she were asleep. Her skin was the same ivory-white of his grandfather's hands.

His grandmother pushed past him and knelt down.

"It's okay, baby," she cooed. "Dr. Crowley's on his way. Everything's going to be okay."

Angel watched her rock back and forth on the floor.

"Is Mommy going to die, too?" he asked in a small voice.

His grandmother glared at him.

"Go and sit with your granddad."

When Dr. Crowley arrived, he pushed the door open without knocking and trudged straight through to the bathroom, trailing clumps of snow behind him.

Angel waited in the living room. He craned his neck

toward the doorway to hear what was happening. They had moved his mother back to her bedroom. The doctor cleaned her up and assured his grandmother that the bleeding had stopped. The two of them stood in the kitchen but Angel could only hear snippets of what was said.

"And you're sure you have no idea who the father was?" came the doctor's tired voice.

"No," his grandmother said. "She wouldn't tell."

Angel could hear her filling the kettle. He leaned further over in the chair. For a long time there was no sound except the warming kettle. Once the water had boiled and the tea was made, they began to speak again. Angel got out of the old recliner and moved toward the kitchen. He rested his head against the door jamb and listened.

"Well, there's no question that she's lost the baby," Dr. Crowley muttered.

"Yes," his grandmother sighed. "It's with the angels now."

The doctor slurped his tea loudly.

"Maybe it's better," his grandmother said. "With all this craziness, maybe it's better."

Angel crept away from the doorway and went to the front hall closet. He took out his and the old man's coats. He tipped his grandfather forward in the chair and slipped his arms into the sleeves. As quietly as he could, he propped open the front door and pushed the wheelchair outside. He waited for a few minutes on the stoop, to see if his grandmother had heard them. When she did not come, he carefully lowered the chair down the steps, and dragged it across the snow-covered lawn.

Angel left his grandfather in the doorway to the woodshed. He went in and found the wings, then set them in the old man's lap. He took a length of rope from the wall and his tarpaulin from under the bench and brought them outside. He put the rope with the wings and covered the lot up with the tarp.

The sidewalks had been cleared of snow and Angel found the push easy at first. It did not get difficult until they'd turned off the main street and headed north, up the hill toward the church. The sidewalk ended just over the crest, beside the cemetery. From there on, Angel had to slog through the slush at the side of the highway. A half mile along they came to the old mine road. No cars had travelled it and the snow was fresh and light. The chair moved easily across its surface.

At the end of the road they came to the path that led to the mine. The old man's head jiggled from side to side as Angel pushed him over the rough ground.

Angel stopped to catch his breath at the end. He left his grandfather in the chair and entered the fenced-in observation deck. Decades of tearing iron ore from the earth had left a massive crater that stretched out in a gigantic oval from the lookout. By the time the mine closed, the pit had reached a depth of some seven hundred and thirty feet.

Angel sat down on the short retaining wall that enclosed the observation deck. It was covered with sloppy graffiti and the floor was littered with beer bottles. Angel kicked a broken neck by his foot, then went to where he had left his grandfather.

There was a gap in the fence beside the lookout and Angel dragged the wheelchair through. He pushed the old man along the top of the crater until he came to a flat, open space. He clicked on the chair's brake and sat on a boulder at the bottom of the tailings.

"The baby's with the angel's now," he said. "Grandma said so."

A line of spittle slipped from the old man's mouth

and Angel got up and wiped it away with his finger. He took the load from his grandfather's lap and put it on the ground. Then he leaned him forward and took off his coat.

"It won't be cold."

Angel sat on the ground and loosened the straps of his backpack. Then he took the rope and got to his feet. He pushed the old man as far back in the chair as he could and wrapped the rope tightly around his chest. He slid one of his grandfather's arms through a shoulder strap and brought the pack over the handle at the back of the chair. Gently, he twisted the other arm backward and pushed it through the second strap. The loose ends of the rope he tied snugly across the middle of the backpack.

When he finished, Angel climbed into his grandfather's lap. He brushed his fingers through the grey-white hair at the front of the old man's head.

"I want you to have my wings, Grandpa," he said, softly.

Angel wiped the last bit of saliva from the old man's chin, then walked to the back of the wheelchair. He released the brake and softly touched the edges of the wings. He leaned forward and whispered into his grandfather's ear.

"You'll be safer with the angels."

A TALK

My father's shotgun lay in the bottom of the boat, on top of the life jackets. Its barrel was dark and oiled, and its pump was pulled back to show the breech empty. The shells were in a small white cardboard box in my lap. I fiddled the lid open and looked at them, then took one out and rolled it in the palm of my hand. Two and a half inches of red plastic tubing, sealed with a paler red at the end to keep the pellets in place. At its base, the shiny copper casing of the blasting cap. It was a pretty thing. More so live than it would be after it was spent. Then it would be an empty husk, smelling of burnt powder, easily blown by the wind.

"Put it back, Michael," my father said. "It's not a toy."

My mother hadn't wanted my father to bring me along. She was already up when he came into my bedroom and shook me awake. And while he was at the stove making scrambled eggs, first for me then himself, she stood watching in the kitchen doorway. I ate my eggs slowly, without talking. My father shovelled his into his mouth as if he didn't want to taste them. After he was done, he went to the hall closet and dug out my coat and boots. My mother followed him and when he turned to come back she stood in front of him, blocking his way. She had her arms folded across her chest.

"Why do you have to take him with you?" she said. "You've never done before."

My father looked at her for a long time but didn't answer. Then he stepped around her and came over to me. He knelt down and slipped my boots onto my feet and wrapped my coat around my shoulders.

"I'll wash up when I get back," he said to my mother.

I had wanted to ask my father the same question my mother had, but didn't. I figured, as he pushed the boat away from the rocky shore and started the motor, that he'd just decided it was time. And I pulled myself tight against the cold morning air and said nothing.

I could hear the echoing cracks of gunfire as my father steered the boat around the point and into the bay. When I turned to him he didn't return my look. What he did was ease off the throttle and gaze out across the water toward the far shoreline. All his concentration was focused there, but I could see nothing except the dim shadows of the trees in the dawn twilight. I felt his hand on my shoulder.

"There they are," he said. "Do you see them?"

I shook my head. To my eyes there was nothing there. Nothing but darkness.

"Listen." He cut the engine. "Hear them?"

A thin whistling touched my ears and suddenly the small flock appeared — four shadows fifteen feet above our heads. I watched them pass over, silhouetted against the blue-grey sky. They flew toward the near shoreline and began a bank that would have brought them back toward us. Out of the corner of my eye I saw flashes in the reed beds along the shore. And I heard the cracks again. The shadows broke quickly to the right and disappeared over the trees.

"Tough luck," my father said. "Teals are hard targets. Very fast birds."

The next thing I heard was a quick breath of wind and the patter sound of hard rain on water. It was very short. Then it came twice more. My father moved to the middle of the boat and put the oars into their locks.

"We'd better get over there," he said and smiled, "before we fill up with shot."

He rowed us toward the reed beds from which the flashes had come. There, nestled in the shallow water, was another boat the same as ours, a fourteen foot Mariner. The only difference was that its shiny metal surface was hidden under a thick coat of dull green paint. Two dark figures stood in it, watching our approach. My father gave the oars one more pull, then lifted them out of the water, and we drifted into the reeds. He turned sideways on the bench so as to face the other boat.

"Jesus Christ," came a voice. "Thought you'd never show up."

"Little late, is all," my father said.

"Surprised you could come at all after last night," another voice said.

"Shut it, Charlie," my father said. "The boy's with me."

It was quiet for a moment. Then a low chuckle drifted its way across the water.

Charlie Gillis and Bob Kord, the two men in the other boat, were friends of my father. I didn't know them all that well. My mother never let them come round to the house. She didn't like them much. And whenever my father mentioned them, she would close up tight like a fist and not say anything. I only ever heard her speak their names twice. The first time she was screaming and throwing dishes at my father. The other she was sitting on the sofa crying. My father wasn't home.

When our boat was close enough, my father and Charlie reached out their hands to one another and pulled the boats side by side. My father took the slack of their anchor-line and tied it off to our bow, locking the two boats together. Then he picked up his shotgun, took the box of shells from my lap and stepped across into the other boat. The three of them huddled together and lit cigarettes. They whispered a few things I couldn't hear, then Bob stepped away and came into our boat with me.

"How you doing there, Mikey?" he said as he sat down beside me on the rear bench and broke open the barrel of his shotgun, sending the two spent cartridges over the side of the boat and into the water. He smiled and fished two new shells from the pocket of his vest and reloaded his gun.

"First time out, eh?" he said.

I nodded and looked across to my father. He was sitting down beside Charlie, still whispering. I heard them laugh.

"You thirsty there, Mikey?" Bob said tapping my arm. He reached inside his jacket and pulled out a thermos and twisted off the cap.

"Here," he said, "take a sip of this. It's bloody cold out here. It'll help."

The coffee was only lukewarm, still it burned as it slid down my throat. I tried not to cough but did anyway.

"Got a little kick to it, eh?" Bob said. "That's the rum," he laughed. "You come out with the big boys, you got to play the same game."

Then he laughed again and slapped me hard on the back. He took a drink himself. I sat still with my hands tucked under the backs of my legs. I wanted my father to come back into our boat and Bob to go back to his. It wasn't that Bob wasn't friendly, he was plenty that.

The few times I'd met him he always had a trick to show me, or a dirty joke that I couldn't tell my mother. But there was something about him I didn't like. Something that frightened me.

He stood up then and snapped the barrel of his gun closed. My father turned when he heard the sound and got back to his feet. He met Bob halfway, the two of them with a foot in each boat, and took a long drink from Bob's thermos. Then he sat down beside me and handed back the box of shells.

"How about you be my ammo-man, Michael?" he said. "It's an important job. Do you think you can handle it?"

I told him that I thought I could, and he ruffled my hair with his hand.

"Good stuff," he said.

We were quiet for a very long time after that. My father and the other two men stared out across the bay toward the far shore. I watched them. They all breathed slowly, and the smoke of their breath hung briefly before their faces, then disappeared into nothing. Around us the sky was beginning to lighten and the late-fall songbirds began their calling in the woods at our backs. A dull mist drifted over the water beyond the reeds. I could feel myself growing tired and let my head sink toward my chest. My father's soft whispers brought it back to level.

"Did your mother talk to you last night?" he said.

I looked at him for a moment, and when he didn't say anything else I shook my head.

"Before she put you to bed," he said, "she didn't say anything to you?"

I shook my head again and told him no.

"I see," he said, then looked out again toward the far shore. His finger played with the safety catch on his gun, flicking it back and forth. He shifted on the bench and I felt the boat rock slightly.

"She was supposed to talk to you last night," he said. "Then I was going to talk to you this morning."

He paused.

"What do you think of hunting so far?" he said.

I said that I thought it was okay. He nodded and wiped his nose on his sleeve.

"It's better when there's more birds," he said.

I told him that I didn't mind.

"Still," he said, "it's more exciting when there is. Best when they come in big flocks. When you don't have to pick any one in particular. You can just let loose without having to worry."

I told him again that I didn't mind. That just sitting there was fine. Then he turned to face me.

"Listen, Michael," he said. "This thing I'm supposed to talk to you about—"

"Birds coming," Charlie whispered hoarsely. "Just below the tree-line."

My father turned away. "I got 'em," he said and rose slowly to his feet.

The ducks were just a blur at first, like a part of the foliage shifting. Then the blur separated into three distinct forms, growing further apart as they approached. When they were about twenty feet out they began their bank. The shooting started. It sounded like cannons going off in my head. The middle duck stopped in mid-flight, as if it had run into something solid. It rose straight up about a foot, then began to tumble head over tail until it hit the water with a thump I felt in my chest. The other two split off in separate directions.

There was a dead silence. Then Charlie laughed, then Bob, and finally my father. Bob slapped his leg and swore. He dug inside his jacket and pulled out his thermos again. I stood up and looked out to where the bird had fallen. It was splashing in the water.

"Well," Charlie said, lighting a cigarette and looking at me, "time for you to earn your wings, kid."

"Yep," Bob said. "That sucker's still trying to fly out there."

My father looked at me and smiled, then walked up to the front of the boat and untied the anchor-line. I fell back onto the bench when Charlie pushed our boat away with his foot. My father sat down in the middle and began to row us out of the reeds. I could feel the cold again and slid my hands back under my thighs. I had to pee. As we got further out, I could see the duck in the water. It was on its side, flapping itself in circles on the surface.

"It's very easy, Michael," my father said after he put up the oars. "Just wring it like it's a dish cloth. Once and it's done. Don't even have to think about what you're doing."

I looked down into the water beside me. The duck was still spinning, its one wing beating furiously and its feet pumping. It was working so hard but getting nowhere. Its eye was black and shiny and looking straight into the sky. I turned back to my father.

"It's better if you don't look at it," he said.

I shook my head. I began to cry. Not hard, but I could feel the warm tears slide down my cheeks. My father got up and came to the back bench beside me. He put his arm around me.

"Look, son," he said. "It's okay. Don't worry."

He pulled my forehead against his cheek and I could feel the rough stubble of his beard. The coffee smelled sweet on his breath.

"Don't worry," he said. "Everything will be okay."

He let go of me and reached over the side of the boat. I watched his shoulders. For a moment they were still, then they jerked quickly and the sound of the splashing stopped. I looked up into the sky then, searching for the other two ducks. The sky was empty.

GREATER POWERS

The Death card had gone missing a few days earlier. At first, Gemma had not been bothered by its disappearance. Things go missing for a reason, she'd told Michael, and things are found for a reason. There are forces more powerful than you and I, she'd said the night it vanished, and it's not for us to question. So Michael sat quietly on the edge of the bed watching television while Gemma tipped everything on end in the lounge.

"You're certain you haven't seen it?" she called through to Michael.

"Greater powers," he shouted back, then leaned forward and raised the volume. He let her bang around until her cursing grew too loud to ignore, then he switched off the television and wandered out of the bedroom. He stood in the doorway of the lounge. The cushions from the settee and the armchairs were piled in the middle of the floor. The coffee table had been pushed to the side of the room and the drawers of the sideboard were pulled wide, their contents strewn across the top.

"Don't just stand there," Gemma huffed. "Help me look."

"I wouldn't know where to start."

She glared at him, then plunged her hand down the side of the smaller armchair. Michael watched the gypsy kerchief slip off her head and fall to the floor. The gaudy colours of her jumper and long skirt danced to the jingling of her silver bracelets as she searched amongst the springs. Unsuccessful, she retreated to the middle of the room, her empty hands clenched in fists at her side.

"I guess you'll have to use something else."

Gemma looked at him stupidly.

"It's the Death card, Michael. The *Death* card. It has immense significance. I cannot use something else."

Michael sucked his teeth and leaned against the door jamb. "Well, if you can't find it, you're going to have to."

An exasperated breath slipped through Gemma's lips and she turned to the cushions once again, lifting them, shaking them, tossing them aside.

"Then cancel the appointment."

"I can't cancel the appointment," Gemma grumbled. "It's Mrs. Barlow. She comes every week. Besides, she's old."

Michael shook his head and moved into the lounge. He went to the sideboard and lazily sifted through the detritus.

"At her age," he said, scattering old birthday and Christmas cards, "she should be happy you lost the bloody thing."

Gemma stopped. "Is that supposed to be funny?"

"No."

"Because I think it's out of order."

"Truth often is."

The buzzer put a halt to further argument.

"Shit. She's early."

They stood and surveyed the carnage. The buzzer sounded again.

"Darling," Gemma said, sweetly, "will you go down and let her in while I straighten up?"

Michael lay on the bed watching Attenborough and his plants on the television, but the soft murmur of Gemma's voice in the next room kept intruding on his concentration. While Sir David hopped from continent to continent in his ever-pale-blue shirt, Michael closed his eyes. In the darkness he could see Gemma again as he first had. It was his first week in England. She was the friend of a friend and sitting beautiful at the table when he entered the pub. Before he'd even sat down he knew he wanted her, the way people know they want the lovely puppies in shop windows. Her hair was long and blonde and fell appealingly onto the black shoulders of her woollen dress. Her voice was sweet and her accent still novel. The bottled scent that swept across the table was an aphrodisiac; it pulled him willingly toward her. The entire evening his eyes rested on the soft whiteness of her neck. They spoke only to one another and he remembered how she ran her fingers softly across his knuckles; and how this simple gesture threw him into a terror of excitement.

Michael opened his eyes and got up from the bed. He slipped into the kitchen and filled the kettle. Gemma's murmuring still played in his ears. He dropped the teabags into the pot and listened. Puppies grow up, he thought, become comfortable and start expecting things. She stopped talking as he poured the water. He waited.

It was Mrs. Barlow's bitter widow's voice that broke through the silence: "And just what is that meant to be?"

"Well..." Michael could hear Gemma flounder. "Actually... it's the Death card."

Again there was silence.

"No it isn't," blurted Mrs. Barlow. "It's a Sainsbury's coupon."

Michael moved through the brief hallway and stood outside the entrance to the lounge. He tipped his head toward the crack of the door.

"I am sorry, Mrs. Barlow," Gemma stammered, "but I seem to have mislaid the actual card."

"I'll say you have. But that, that is simply ridiculous."

"You must understand, Mrs. Barlow," Gemma continued, "that the importance lies in what the card represents."

The old woman puffed loudly. "As far as I'm concerned, the only thing that represents is 10p off tinned ravioli."

Michael smiled and pushed through the door. Both women stopped and turned to look at him.

"Anyone for tea?" he asked. "I've just made a pot."

Gemma stared at him, the blankness in her face complete.

"Have you seen this?"

"What's that, Mrs. Barlow?"

"This, this," she said, and leaned her aging bulk forward and picked up the offending scrap of paper.

"Yes," Michael said. "I believe I cut it from the paper."

"But do you know what it is?"

"My guess would be a coupon for ravioli."

"Not according to your wife."

"Oh?"

"Yes. According to her, it's the Death card." She gave the coupon a disagreeable shake, then let it flutter back to the table.

"Really?" Michael said, giving his head a scratch. "Well, I should think that's quite possible."

"I beg your pardon?" Mrs. Barlow burped.

"Why not?" Michael continued. "I mean, in lieu of the actual Death card, I think it a quite suitable replacement. After all, the significance is in the representation, not the appearance. Isn't that right, *darling*?"

Gemma cleared her throat. "I was just saying as much."

"Well," Michael smiled. "There you have it."

Mrs. Barlow pulled her tired, lumpy body out of the deep armchair and straightened her mourning dress.

"Forgive me if I don't accept your opinion, Mr. Farrel," she said, in a slow angry voice. "But your wife tells me you've no faith in the cards."

"Quite true, Mrs. Barlow. Quite true." Michael smiled again. "As far as I'm concerned, it's a load of bunk."

Gemma let out an embarrassed whimper and an unpleasant guttural effusion slipped from the blue-haired Mrs. Barlow.

"Right," he said. "Who's for tea?"

Michael stood on the far side of the room and watched Gemma undress for bed. She pulled the loose jumper over her head; it caught her hair up then let it fall across her face. As she brushed it away, Michael stared at her breasts, held firm within her brassiere. His eyes remained fixed as she stepped out of her long skirt. He slowly unbuttoned his shirt while Gemma slipped out of her knickers, then unhooked her bra. She stood naked beside the bed for a moment, surveying the discarded clothing, then slid quickly under the covers. Michael held Gemma's nakedness in his mind. It had not changed. It was the same body which had so captured him when he'd first seen her, first touched her. Nothing had drooped or sagged; nothing had grown fatter or hairier. The breasts were still hard, the stomach flat, the buttocks still round and smooth. It was the same, exactly the same. He watched her settle into her habitual position, then dropped his boxers and climbed into bed.

"The headmaster came into my lesson again today," he said, shrinking away from her icy feet.

"Does that bother you?"

"Well, it does seem to be happening more often."

"I meant my putting my feet on you."

"Oh, no. Not at all. They're just a little cold."

"I wouldn't worry about the head," Gemma said, curling toward him. "He's only doing his job. I'm sure he sits in on other lessons."

"Maybe."

"You're a wonderful teacher," she whispered, softly kissing his ear.

"I don't know." Michael shifted away slightly. "He did mention the detentions again."

"What did he say?" she asked, keeping pace with his movements.

"He made some crack about my going for a new record."

Michael had reached the edge of the bed.

"You have to admit, Michael, fifty-six in one day is rather excessive."

He turned unwillingly to face her. "That's what I mean. If I had any control whatsoever, I wouldn't have to give so many. I think he knows that."

Gemma slipped her hand between his thighs. "Forget about him."

Michael tipped his head back as she began to fondle him. He closed his eyes. There was no point in resisting. He'd tried before, but her tenacity was shattering. Instead, he conjured. First a face, then the body to which it belonged. She was one of his sixth form students. He blocked out her name. It was of no interest to him. All he wanted was the body. The long, pale legs that crawled from under her short, dark skirt.

The young, growing breasts held tightly by the creamy blouse. The dangling, ginger curls that fell across the freckles of her wide face. The ice-blue eyes that held nothing and asked for nothing. And while Michael held the two bodies — the young girl's in his mind, Gemma's in his arms — he tried to remember when it had all started, when the imaginings had begun. It was not recent. Nor was there any pattern to it, save that each body was new to him. They belonged to fellow teachers, students, parents of students; or women he'd seen in shops, on the television, in newspapers and magazines. It did not matter. None were repeated. They came once and were banished. And none were Gemma.

Michael was still awake long after Gemma's breathing had become deep and laboured in its customary snore. Lying on his back, staring at the ceiling, he tried to slow his own breathing to match hers — a tactic he knew to be hopeless. Her dreambound tics and shudders taunted him. When the insomnia first started it was usually after they'd had sex. Then it began to happen regularly. Every night. He grew almost to anticipate it. He would stare through the darkness above him and imagine things differently. Sometimes he would have himself walk into some other pub; other times he thought about a life in which he'd never left home, never come to England; and in a few instances he dreamt of waking up alone. This particular bout, however, was rife with a different sort of contemplation. Exodus, chapter twenty, verses one through seventeen, swirled about his head: the next morning's lesson. In six hours he would stand before the vacuous faces of 8A RE and deliver unto them the laws of God, as Moses had to the Israelites. But, lying naked beside Gemma, the sweat dried from both their bodies, he wandered sleeplessly through the commandments, wondering how many he had broken. How many that day. How many that night.

Michael rolled over and looked into Gemma's snoring face. Her mouth was opened wide and her sour breath forced its way deep into his nostrils. He could feel the aroma tugging at his nasal hairs and prodding his uvula. Very slowly, he stretched out his arms and took her throat in his hands.

He opened his eyes to an empty bed and smiled, then slid his hand over to Gemma's side of the mattress. It was still warm. He rolled away and pulled the pillow over his head. He could hear her moving about in the kitchen. She was singing, but the tune and lyrics were too muffled to recognize. He pushed the pillow tighter against his ears.

"Rise and shine," she sang from the bedroom doorway.

Her lilting voice dug its way through the pillow's stuffing. Michael rolled onto his back and looked at her. Gemma had already bathed and dressed. She stood before him looking as fresh and clean as she did at midday. She carried the smell of frying bacon into the room with her.

"Rise and shine," she sang again, then turned and went back to the kitchen.

Michael lay there until he knew it was too late to have a proper shower and shave. Then he pulled himself slowly from under the duvet and went into the toilet. He turned on the faucet and splashed cold water on his face, then did the same to his armpits. After he towelled off he ran a brush through his hair and squeezed toothpaste onto his tongue. His red-rimmed eyes stared back at him from the mirror and squinched at the sound of Gemma's incessant trillings.

Back in the bedroom he pulled on the previous day's clothes, then went through to the kitchen. Gemma was just licking the last of the bread crumbs from the corner of her mouth. There were two bacon and tomato butties set out for him. Michael poured himself a cup of tea and sat down at the table just as Gemma was getting up.

"You're up early," he said, taking a sip of tea.

"Yes. You haven't seen my coat have you?" she asked, and walked out of the kitchen without waiting for a reply.

Michael took another sip from his cup and stared at the butties before him. With his finger, he pushed one to the edge of the plate and over. When he heard her coming back toward the kitchen, he put it back into place.

"Found it," she said.

"Good."

Gemma stood before him and pulled on her coat, flicking her hair free from the collar. She smiled at him queerly, then leaned forward and took a slurp of his tea.

"I had the strangest dream last night," she said, furrowing her brow.

"Really?" Michael took the cup from her. "Do tell."

"It was truly bizarre." Gemma absently buttoned her coat as she spoke. "In it, the dream, I was the last woman in England to be executed. Don't ask me why I was the last, I just know I was."

"Uh-huh." Michael began to slide the buttie toward the edge of the plate again. "That is strange."

"Well," she continued, "that's not the strangest part. Yes, it's strange enough, but there's more."

"Something exciting, I hope."

The buttie fell off the plate.

"Depends on how you look at it, I guess." Gemma picked up the buttie and took a bite. "I didn't think so."

She chewed slowly, then began to search the pockets of her coat while Michael waited.

"You *are* going to tell me?" he said.

"Yes, of course." She paused again, to collect her thoughts. "Right. So, there I was, in the gallows. Standing over the door. The noose around my neck. I could actually feel it, the noose. It was all frighteningly real. Anyway, I turned to the hangman and asked him why. Why was I to be the last woman executed in England. Do you know what he said to me?"

Michael shook his head.

"He said." Gemma lowered her voice. "He said, *for the willful and deliberate murder of Michael P Farrel.*" She shivered. "And the thing that really frightened me was that he sounded like you."

"Who?"

"The hangman. Who else?"

Michael stared at her, a small, grim smile forming on his lips.

"Well, I suppose it is rather funny," Gemma said.

"Yes. Quite."

"So, that was my queer dream."

"It certainly was."

"What do you suppose it means?" she asked, finishing off the buttie.

"I'm sure I wouldn't know," Michael chuckled. "Best ask Dr. Freud about that."

"Or my cards."

"Right. Or your cards."

Gemma plunged her hands deep into her coat pockets, this time leaving them there. She walked over to Michael and leaned over to be kissed. He gave her a quick peck on the cheek, then one on the nose. She gave him a big toothy grin in return.

"I'm off," she said.

"Where to?"

"Town."

"For?"

"New cards, of course."

"Of course."

"The old ones aren't much good without you-know-what," she said, as she left the kitchen.

"Not much good at all," Michael said, quietly to her back.

She called *ta-ra* from the door then was gone from the flat like she'd been gone from bed when he'd awoken; vanished, save for the lingering smell of bacon. Michael looked down at the remaining buttie, then got up from the table and deposited it in the bin under the sink. He headed into the lounge to collect his things. Gemma had scattered his exercise books the night before, so he bundled them up and dropped them into his briefcase. His blazer still lay in a clump in the corner where he'd tossed it the day before.

His work tucked safely away, he crossed to where his jacket lay. He paused before picking it up and looked about the room. Except for the exercise books and his blazer, Gemma had left no trace of the previous night's chaos. Everything was back in its proper place as if nothing had happened.

THE WHISPERING LADY

— for Daniel and Jessica

Eamon Maguire slipped up the back stairs and into his flat unnoticed by Mrs. Flannery. He locked the door behind him, then turned and fell over the rubbish strewn across his path. The sledgehammer crashed to the floor. He froze, listening for movement from downstairs. There was none. He got back to his feet, switched on the light and picked his way through to the lounge. From the flooded ashtray he rescued a half-smoked joint and relit it. The newspaper still lay open on the settee, stained greasy at the edges where his fingers had held it. The smoke burnt through his nose as he laughed at the headline: "Moving Madonna Puts Barrow with Knock and Asdee."

He took another hit off the joint then squeezed the ember onto the floor and crushed it into the carpet with his heel. His head began to spin as he flopped down on the settee and kicked off his boots. The stench of his socks filled the room. He bent forward and pulled one off, then used it to cover the mouthpiece of the telephone. He had to hold his breath while he waited for his brother to answer.

"Hello."

"That you, Father Maguire?" Eamon said, through the rank sock.

"Yes. Who is this?" came the priest's tired voice. "Have you any idea the time?"

"Take a look at your precious statue now," Eamon said.

And he hung up.

The whole of Barrow was at Our Lady of the Blessed Heart by the time Eamon got there late the next morning. They were crowded round the small grotto at the foot of the hill on which the church sat. Eamon chuckled to himself and began to push his way through. At the front, a yellow rope separated the onlookers from the rubble that used to be the Shifting Lady of Barrow.

Eamon tried to keep the smile from his lips as he looked at the astonished faces. There were low mutters of disgust and whimpers of disbelief. He could feel a laugh start to build in his belly, like a fart that had to be let loose regardless of company. Instead, he turned to Jacko Bell, who'd just stepped up to the rope beside him. Jacko was old and smelled foul.

"What's the fuss, Jacko?"

"What do you think?" the old man said, as he wiped his ever-dripping nose. "Some twat smashed the Lady."

"Well, what do you think of that?" Eamon said, and felt free to expel his chortle.

"Ah, piss off," Jacko grunted and turned back into the crowd.

On the far side of the rabble Eamon could see his brother talking to a young man in a gleaming suit with hair to match. The notepad gave the young man away and Eamon began to make his way across. He checked his mirth and offered nods of understanding to the keening of shameful and pity that poured from the bystanders. Halfway across he looked up into the face of Mary Delaney. He hadn't expected to see her there. Especially not with puffy eyes and cheeks stained with wet mascara. Eamon pushed past before she could say anything or see his face flush. When he reached his brother he flashed him a wide, satisfied grin.

"I don't see as there's anything to smile at, Eamon," the young priest said.

"Now that's no tone to take with your brother, father."

Eamon could tell that the disclosure of their fraternal bond was irksome. Yet, if he hadn't made the revelation it would never have been apparent. Eamon was tall and lanky with an ever-present stubble mottling his gaunt cheeks. He dressed for function, and for him that precluded both coordination and cleanliness. Hugh, the good father, was his polar opposite. His black trousers perfectly matched his black shirts. And where Eamon's hair hung in long oily strings, the priest's was cut close to the scalp. It made Eamon swell to know that this list of incongruities was being registered by the newspaperman as he stood there.

"So, father," the reporter began again, "this can't do much for Barrow's hope of becoming the next Knock."

"True, it's a setback," the priest said.

"And you've no idea who might be responsible?"

"Pretty obvious, if you ask me," Eamon broke in. Both men stopped. "Well, it's a Dubliner, for certain."

The reporter cleared his throat. "Really? A Dubliner? Why would you say that, now?"

"Jealousy, pure and simple." Eamon felt the joy rumble in his guts again. "Got no meccas of their own, and they're bitter about it."

"That'll do, Eamon."

"Just telling your man here what he wants to know, father."

Father Maguire turned his back on his brother and started to explain that, when it came down to it, it didn't matter *who'd* exacted the horrible deed, but *why*. The person, or persons, were obviously in need of guidance. This was not a cry of anger, but a call for help. And at such a trying time, Christian morality should not be given over to rage.

"Forgiveness," the young priest said, "is the keystone of the Church. And that should not be forgotten."

"So true, Padre," Eamon said, as he forced a shoulder, then himself, back into the conversation. "So true. Now tell me, when are you going to clean this lot up?"

"Yes," said the gleaming reporter. "What about that? Will you rebuild the shrine?"

"No, no," said Father Maguire in the voice he usually saved for the pulpit. "Whole or in pieces, she is still Our Lady. And though her body is destroyed, her spirit is undamaged. She'll remain where she lies."

"You're not leaving that pile of rubble there?" Eamon said, too loudly.

His brother turned on him quickly. "That's enough out of you, yeah. You don't care about any of this, so why don't you just shove off."

Eamon smiled at the two men and turned back into the crowd.

"Prick," he muttered.

Jimmy Magillicuddy got up and went into the toilet after telling Eamon to give it a couple of minutes and meet him there. So Eamon finished his pint, asked Denny behind the bar to start him another and headed into the gents'. He thought it was empty until he heard a whisper come at him through a half-opened stall door.

"What are you doing, Jimmy?" Eamon said. "Gone a little espionage, don't you think?"

Magillicuddy pushed the door open wider. "What do you expect, Eamon?" he said. "We're in a public place."

Eamon pulled him out of the stall. "Ah, for Christ's sake. If you can deal it on the work site in front of the whole friggin' world, there's no sense hiding in the shitter now."

Magillicuddy looked confused for a moment, then shrugged his shoulders. "Truth in that," he said, and pulled a clear plastic bag from the front pocket of his grimy jeans. "Give us fifteen."

"Fuck that," Eamon said. "You'll get ten."

"Fair enough," Magillicuddy answered, without missing a beat. "Then you can treat me to a smoke. Got any skins?"

"I do," Eamon said, and snatched the bag from his hand. "And if you don't mind, I'll do the rolling." He pulled cigarette papers from his back pocket, opened a sheet and sprinkled the weed along its length.

"Ah, Jesus, man. Not in here. Take it to the car park."

Eamon's pint was waiting for him when he got back to the bar. He slipped onto the stool and gulped down half to clear the thickness of the pot from his palate. The smoke not only stoned him but made him feel generous, so he told Denny to pour one for Jimmy, who sat down beside him.

"So," Magillicuddy said, "what do you make of this statue business?"

Eamon set his glass down and looked at him suspiciously. "What're you saying?"

Magillicuddy looked as if he'd been caught out doing something illicit. It was a look that visited him every time he smoked and often when he didn't.

"Just figured it's pretty big news," he sputtered.

"And what's it got to do with me?"

"Well," Magillicuddy said, "your brother being the priest and all."

"He could be the fucking pope and it's still got nothing to do with me."

"Just a shame, I'm saying."

"Why?" spat Eamon. "You go down there a lot, do you?"

"No," said Magillicuddy. "Never."

"Then shut it."

The brief calm that the smoke had brought left Eamon. He rapped his knuckles on the bar and motioned to Denny to pour him another. The thought of his brother turning his back on him to speak to the reporter fuelled the rage that Magillicuddy's talk had kindled. He sat and waited for his new pint, his mind bubbling with hostility at his brother's glowing, goading face.

"What was that?" he said sharply to Magillicuddy.

"What?"

"What did you just say?"

The anxiety the grass had stirred up in Jimmy transmogrified into perfect bewilderment. "Nothing," Jimmy said. "I didn't say nothing."

"You did," Eamon muttered fiercely. "You just whispered something at me."

"On the Bible, Eamon," Magillicuddy swore. "I didn't say a word."

"Your pint, lad." Denny passed the glass across the bar.

"Fuck it!" Eamon shouted. "Give it to him."

And walked out of the pub.

Eamon heard the whispering again as he walked into the house and yelled at Mrs. Flannery, who had been sitting peacefully in the downstairs lounge reading her cookbooks. The look of fright that settled on her face lightened his mood. He detested his landlady. She was nosy, fat and mothering — three things he could not abide. She put up with his surliness, his filth and his noise because it gave her a sense of security. She'd told Eamon that she felt safer with a man in the house again; it was a comfort to know that he was just up the stairs. Eamon was grateful that Mr. Flannery'd had the foresight to put deadbolts on the doors at the top of the front and back staircases before he'd died. Mrs. Flannery had not been allowed upstairs since Eamon had moved in. Neither had she been while her husband was still alive. So Eamon did not doubt her when she said his being there reminded her of her dear dead Sean. Nor did he care.

After a quick, insincere apology, Eamon bounded up the stairs and slammed and locked the door behind him. The stink of rotten takeout struck him as he switched on the light. He stood still in the middle of the lounge and listened. Satisfied he could hear nothing, save the eternal ticking of the beetles in the rafters, he walked over to the portable stereo and slipped in a cassette. The thump of hard rock filled the air.

He pulled the clear plastic bag of weed from his back pocket and held it up to the light. "Good dope," he said aloud, then slipped out a skin. He rolled a spliff and sat down on the settee. As he leaned forward to light it, a cold breeze blew up the back of his untucked shirt. He sat up with a chill and looked to the window. It was closed. He bent over again and, as he struck the match, once more felt the draft. He turned his head slowly to the window, then the pain seared his fingertips.

"Jesus fuck!" he hollered and dropped the match to the floor. He stuck his finger and thumb into his mouth and sucked on the sulfur brand. He looked at the joint in his other hand then dropped it onto the coffee table.

"Real good dope," he said, and got up and went into the bedroom without switching off the tape.

On the bench outside the newsagent's, Eamon sat and looked at the article. There was no photograph, which pleased him because it would nettle his brother. He bit into a Wispa and began to read. The story was as bland as the reporter had been burnished. He sniggered at the chronicle of dismay and disgust, and smiled openly at "Suspicion Lies with Discontented Dubliners." His grin vanished, however, when he saw the claim attributed to Father Hugh Maguire.

"Bastard," he muttered.

"Well, that puts us on the map, I'd say."

Eamon spun around into the poxy face of Declan Bone. He hadn't seen Bone since he'd finished his last stretch of work and he'd no desire to see him again until his next. Declan parked his heavy body on the bench next to Eamon and flashed the gap-toothed smile that was the least appealing of his features, next to his ravaged complexion.

"How do, Pussee?" Eamon said.

"I wish you wouldn't call me that, Maguire," Bone said, with obvious hurt.

"Why not? It's got character."

"Still."

"Suit yourself," Eamon said, and carried on reading. He went back over the section he'd just finished as Bone watched over his shoulder. "What a load of shite."

"True," Bone chirped. "It's shameful."

Eamon gave him a stupid look. "I'm talking about the article, Pussee."

"Oh," Bone nodded. "I wouldn't know. Don't read the papers."

"Here." Eamon pointed at the story. "Look at this." He read the quotation in disgust.

"Yes," Bone said, and nodded again. "He's got a good head on his shoulders, that brother of yours."

"Did you hear what I said, you eejit?" Eamon

stabbed his finger into the paper. "I said that."

"It's funny, that," Bone continued. He sounded pleased with himself. "How siblings think alike. Like my cousin and me. There's got to be something in that. Do you not think?"

"No!" shouted Eamon, as he punched the paper. "No, I don't, you dozy bastard. Because *he* didn't think nothing, and *he* didn't say nothing. I stood there, right beside him, and said it. *Me*. Not *him*."

"Well, there you go."

"What?"

"Proves my point, that does." Bone's big rotten smile opened his face again.

Eamon shook his head. "You're a real twat, you know that, Pussee?"

"What? What?"

"Just shut your ugly hole," Eamon said, and got up from the bench. As he turned to walk away, he flicked a 'V' at Bone's back. "Fat git," he said, under his breath.

"That's not very Christian now, is it, Eamon?"

Eamon looked up to see his brother on the pavement in front of him.

"Christ," he mumbled.

"No, just his servant, I'm afraid. And lucky for you, I'm sure." Then he turned to Bone. "Hello, Declan."

"Father."

He looked back to Eamon. "Off to work, are you?"

"Actually, Hugh, I'm between jobs right now."

"Oh, I see," said the priest. "Doing your stint as a state beneficiary again."

"That time of the year, you know."

Father Maguire massaged his brow. "Eamon, son. When are you going to get yourself sorted? Get a real job? Get a haircut? Start taking some pride?"

"It's a funny thing there, Hugh," Eamon said calmly. "I could've sworn Ma was dead."

The priestly mask slipped quickly from his brother's face.

"father," Bone called from the bench. "That's a wonderful bit in the papers there."

"Yes," Father Maguire said, through an instant grin. "Quite impressive. In fact, I've come down to pick up a few more copies."

"You must be pleased with its accuracy," Eamon said.

"I beg your pardon?"

"Well, you were spot on with your suspicions."

"Ah well, you can't always believe what you read," the priest chuckled. "At any rate I think this whole unsavoury incident may be for the best. The way things are shaping up, with the press and all, we may just bump Knock and Asdee out of the race, after all. Yes," he smiled, "when all is said and done, this'll probably set us right on top of the heap."

"Brilliant," Eamon said.

Eamon carried on down the road without breaking stride until he came to the edge of the village. There he stopped in front of the house in which he and the good father had been children. It had once been a deep purple, but its paint had bleached into a peeling ash-grey. The greater part of the roof had caved in and lay on the floor of the second storey. The front and back gardens were a tangle of unkempt weeds and shards of glass that had been kicked from the windows by bored kids. The bed and breakfast sign was still nailed to the wall outside the front door, but it was barely legible through the carvings of love and swastikas.

Eamon pushed open the front door and picked his way through the wash of lager cans, whiskey bottles, crisp wrappers and other refuse that littered the floor.

He went into the lounge. The room smelled distinctly of shit and rot. He sat down on the darkened windowsill and lit a cigarette. His mother had taken over the running of the B&B after the death of her parents. It was in this room, when it was covered in brocade and lace and lit with supple warmth, that she'd seduced Hugh's father, whom she loved, and Eamon's, whom she did not. Both men had paid their bills and left as their schedules dictated, but there was never any doubt about which of the two was more coveted in his mother's mind. She'd made certain of that. Be proud, she would tell Hugh, like your father. To Eamon, who trailed behind her with his short trousers and a wanting smile, she spoke only with the back of her hand.

On the front step again he took a deep breath of clean air. As a child he'd always hated the house: its closeness and its strangers, its rooms in which he was allowed and the many which were forbidden. He took pleasure in its decay. He flipped his burning cigarette into the twisted garden then turned and spat on the sign. He grinned as his sputum slid thickly through the carvings.

The rest of the day was spent with Magillicuddy and pints and snooker at the Station Inn. Eamon, comfortable in the pub's stable confines, moved the cue-ball every time Magillicuddy turned his back. Whenever possible, he also cheated him out of points. They played their way through nine frames and as many pints. When time was called, Eamon enforced his "Loser Pays" rule and headed back to his flat.

He heard the voice while he was pissing. When he turned to look he sprayed the towels hanging beside the toilet. Then, without doing himself up, he stormed out of the loo. First he thundered into the lounge, then the bedroom. Both were empty. He grabbed his flies as he burst through the door and down the stairs.

"Goddammit!" he bellowed as he descended. "How many times have I told you, woman? Stay out of my place." There was no reply. "Did you hear me? I said, stay the fuck out!"

The main floor of the house was quiet. He walked through the lounge and into the cramped mouldiness of the kitchen. He stuck his head into the even mouldier back bedroom, then came through to the front hall and peeked into the empty closet. He heard the key slide into the door and stepped back into the shadows just as Mrs. Flannery struggled in.

"Where were you?" Eamon hissed.

The widow leapt back in fright and dropped both her keys and purse in favour of an instinctive clutch at her heart. "Jesus, Mary and Joseph, Eamon. You gave me a scare."

"I said, *where* were you?"

"What a silly question," she answered, catching her breath. "You know it's my bingo night."

"And you're just coming in now?"

"I'm a little later than usual, I know. Me and the girls stopped off at the chippy."

"I suppose you didn't just come from upstairs, then?"

"What?" Eamon's intimidation brought a glow of nostalgia to Mrs. Flannery's nervousness. "Of course not. I wouldn't dream of going upstairs. I don't belong there, I know that."

Eamon stared at her, then began to back his way up the stairs.

"Are you all right, dear?" she asked.

"Why wouldn't I be?"

"I don't know," she said. "You just seem a little troubled."

"Bad pint's all," he said, quickly.

He closed the door on her concern. The flat was cold and his head was awash with drink. He went directly into the bedroom and slipped under the covers, still wearing his clothes and boots. He could feel a breeze against his face. He closed his eyes tight and held his breath. In the darkness, he could hear the staccato passage of air through moving lips. He pulled his pillow close around his head.

The next afternoon, when he awoke with what felt like breath in his ear, Eamon promised himself to steer clear of pubs and people. For as long as he could, he remained in the flat. But the stench finally forced him out and he wandered. He passed O'Dwyer's, the Station Inn, Flynn's Tavern. He passed the church and the coaches that were parked at the bottom of the hill. And when he found himself ranging back toward the B&B he stopped and headed for the off-licence. With four cold cans of lager and the newspaper under his arm, he walked back to his flat.

He spread the paper out on the settee and flipped through until he found the headline: "Pilgrims Surge to Shattered Lady." Then he picked up the sledgehammer and smashed it into the article. He felt one of the supports give way beneath the cushions.

The first can of lager foamed over onto his trousers before he could get it to his lips. Once there, it was dispatched without pause. He crushed the empty can against his forehead and immediately opened the second.

The whisper of air escaping the can was unmistakable. Eamon slowly set it down and picked up the next. He held it closer and carefully pulled the tab. Again the indisputable sound. Then the fourth, even nearer his ear. The murmur was clear: *Why?*

His heart beat a tympani in his chest as he looked at the three full cans on the table in front of him. He stared at them, his body as still as stone. The sensations of his bladder filling and his bowels loosening, along with the chill that had poured into the room, made it difficult to remain continent. It wasn't until the sweat rose on his brow that he realized he hadn't taken a breath since he'd opened the last can. The burst of air smashed through his fear and he leapt from the settee and ran.

Eamon didn't stop running until he reached O'Dwyer's. He pushed his way through to the bar and ordered a pint and a whiskey. Magillicuddy's slap on the back nearly sent him over the counter.

"Little jumpy there, Eamon," Magillicuddy said. "Someone after you?"

"You piss off," he growled. "You and your dope can piss right off."

"Keep it down, will you," Magillicuddy said, eyes flicking left and right. "I don't need it broadcast."

"Fuck off," Eamon shot back and quickly swallowed the whiskey. Magillicuddy muttered the same and trudged back to where he'd been sitting. Eamon felt a sudden need to go after him and tell him what his bad pot had done, but he knew he hadn't smoked any that day. Then he saw Mary Delaney on the far side of the pub. The last time he'd spoken to her he'd told her to take a flying fuck and kicked her out of his flat. That had been a month earlier. But a month was a long time, Eamon figured, and Mary, not being an overly attractive girl, was quick to forgive those who'd wronged her. So he picked up his pint, crossed to where she stood, and took her by the elbow.

"Eh? What's this?" Mary blurted.

"Mary," Eamon said breathlessly. "I've got to talk to you."

"You're hurting my arm," she said, through clenched teeth.

"Sorry." Eamon released her elbow. There was a long silence as he slouched before her.

"Well?"

"Ah, you're looking fine, Mary," Eamon said, with his greatest sincerity. "When I saw you the other day at... at the church, I said to myself..."

"Piss off, Eamon."

"Mary?"

"You're a prick, you know that?"

"But I miss you, dear," Eamon gushed. He was used to lying to Mary. He took a gulp of his pint and looked straight into her wide, splotchy face, something he hadn't even liked to do when he'd been seeing her.

"Come on, love," he whispered sweetly. "We had some good times."

"Maybe you did," she said bitterly. "I sure as fuck didn't."

"Mary, Mary, how about—"

"Eamon," she cut him off, "what do you want?"

He'd got her where he wanted. Angry or not, she was ready to listen. But suddenly it all seemed so ridiculous. He took another drink and began to regret having come over to her.

"If you're after getting a shag, think again," she laughed. "I'm with Francis Leahy now." She pointed over her shoulder to a table near the wall.

Eamon looked over and tipped his pint to Francis, who looked back menacingly.

"Fat Frankie," he said to Mary. "Good catch."

"A hell of a lot better than you," she smirked. "Besides, he's going places."

"Right. Straight into the *Guinness Book of Records* if he don't soon stop munching up his Da's dosh."

"Jealous?" Mary said triumphantly.

"Of that fat ponce?" Eamon sniggered.

"Goodbye, Eamon."

"No, wait!" A flush of panic washed over him. "I'm sorry. Really, I am. I mean, it's good, you and Fa...you and Francis." He felt suddenly nervous and the moisture left his mouth and re-emerged in beads on his forehead. He took another long swig of his pint, which slid down his throat without offering any relief. "I need your help, Mary," he said, too quickly.

She looked at him, a slight trace of concern revealing itself around her eyes. Eamon could feel a full confession begin to build somewhere just below his Adam's apple and he tried to force it back down with the last of his beer.

"I've done something," he sputtered.

After a long silence Mary, in a strangely maternal voice, said, "What is it, Eamon? Tell me."

"Well," Eamon began, and tried to hold back the admission. His mind swirled. The last thing he'd intended was a full disclosure. "Someone's... I mean... no. I think..."

"Eamon," Mary said, carefully. "What kind of trouble did you get yourself into?"

"Come to my flat." The words leapt out before Eamon knew what they were.

"What?"

"Yeah, yeah." His mind raced. "Come to my flat. That'll solve it."

"Jesus, Eamon. What are you on about?"

"You come to my flat, then you can tell me if I'm right or not. You can tell me if I'm a nutter."

"I can tell you that right here," she said, growing hard again.

"Come on." He took her by the arm.

"Leggo," Mary hissed, and pulled herself free. "I told you already, I'm with Francis now."

"Look," Eamon seethed. "I don't give a shite about Fatty." Then, almost pleading: "You've got to come, Mary. I need you."

"Why, Eamon?" she said. "Why? So you can talk me out of my pants?"

"Christ, no. It's nothing like that. I just need you to help me."

Once again her bitterness softened. "What's there, Eamon? What is it you want me to see?"

Eamon looked into her broad, poxy face and searched out her eyes. Then, in a low tremulous voice, "I think it's...a woman."

"A what?"

"A woman," he said, slightly louder.

"You prick!" Mary shouted.

"What?"

"You fucking prick!" she yelled again and her voice cracked.

"Jesus Christ, Mary," Eamon said. "What's this all about?"

"Just piss off," she muttered, and turned and walked away.

"Fuck me, then," Eamon said to himself, and began to push his way back to the bar. Halfway there he felt a tap on his shoulder. He turned around and Francis Leahy stood before him. It was then he realized that Francis wasn't so much fat as massive. A good eight inches taller and over a foot wider.

"What did you say to upset my Mary?" Francis growled.

Eamon looked up into his face, which was even more expansive than Mary's. The first thing that came to his mind was the two of them made a perfect match: both equally unbecoming.

"I asked you what you said to my Mary," Francis repeated.

"I heard you."

"Well?"

"It's none of your goddamn business," Eamon said and turned back toward the bar. Francis's hand spun him round again.

"I'm making it my business."

"Fine," Eamon said, through a grin. "I said she'd found herself a nice thick wallet, but it was too bad she had to shag such a spotty, fat cunt to get it."

The next thing Eamon felt was Francis's meaty fist mashing into his face, and all went black.

Through the darkness Eamon could see Magillicuddy sitting on the bonnet of a car, a cigarette glowing between his lips.

"I'll bet that hurt," Jimmy chuckled.

Eamon sat up and brushed the car park gravel from his hair, then carefully touched the swollen spot above his right eye. The lump was enormous; he could feel Francis's knuckle marks across his brow. Then he remembered the voice that had woken him.

"Did you say something to me?" he asked Magillicuddy harshly.

"Say," Jimmy mocked. "Thanks for dragging me out of there after I was thick enough to get thumped by the biggest bugger in the joint."

"I asked," Eamon threatened, "if you said something while I was lying here?"

"Sure," Magillicuddy said, and angrily threw away his cigarette. "I called your name a couple of times."

"But now?" Eamon snapped. "Just before I sat up?"

Jimmy shrugged. "Naw, I thought you were dead. I was just going to finish my fag and head back in."

"Fuck me," Eamon muttered and rubbed his head again.

Magillicuddy took out his cigarettes and offered one to Eamon.

"You're acting pretty weird, Eamon," he said. "I mean, you've always been a little fucked-up, no offense, but now you're just getting plain weird."

Eamon looked up at him. He didn't really like Magillicuddy, but he disliked him less than most others. He did have a big mouth, though. But now that Mary was out of the question, it didn't seem to him that he had any other option. He reluctantly lifted himself up and sat next to Magillicuddy.

"Jimmy," he said. "Listen to me."

Magillicuddy didn't like the confidential tone of his voice and immediately shrank away. Now that Eamon was up off the ground and within striking distance, Jimmy began to regret having called him fucked-up and weird. The rodent twitch he'd tried to control his whole life overtook his limbs.

"What?" he asked, nervously.

"Will you quit fucking fidgeting," Eamon said sharply.

Magillicuddy did his best.

"Right," Eamon went on. "I've got something to tell you."

"Oh no," Magillicuddy said. He got up from the car bonnet and started to pace. "I don't want to hear nothing." Jimmy knew how poorly he could keep secrets. "Whatever you got to say, Eamon, don't. Tell it to someone else."

Eamon flicked his cigarette at Magillicuddy, who switched directions like a shooting-gallery duck when it hit him.

"What do you think I just tried, you twat?" he said. "Look what that got me."

Jimmy stopped and looked at Eamon's eye.

"He got you good," he chirped in a vain attempt to

switch the topic. "Heard it all the way across the pub, I did. Smack. Thought you were dead before you hit the floor."

"Jimmy, son," Eamon said, slowly. "You're going to listen to me."

"Ah, Christ, Maguire. Please don't. You know I can't keep my mouth shut."

Eamon got up and stood close to Magillicuddy. "The important thing, Jimmy," he said, straight into his face, "is that you know that. And knowing is half the battle." Then he took a breath and lowered his voice. "Besides, if you don't keep your gob shut, I'll make what Fat Frankie did to me look like a fucking kiss."

"You see," Magillicuddy yelped. "You know I can't keep it shut. You know I'll blab."

"I'm telling you, Jimmy," Eamon said, quietly. "And you will keep your mouth shut. Right?"

"I'm not going to listen," Magillicuddy protested.

"You are."

They both knew that was the final word on the matter. Jimmy resigned himself to the fact, and in doing so, calmed considerably.

"Gimme another fag," Eamon said, and sat on the car again. Magillicuddy obeyed. Eamon lit it and inhaled deeply. "I think I'm freaking out," he said matter-of-factly. "I'm hearing things. Weird stuff, like you said."

Jimmy chuckled. "It's the dope, man."

Eamon shook his head.

"Sure it is," Magillicuddy continued, relief in his voice. "It's really powerful shite. Panama Red. Definitely worth fifteen."

"It's not the pot, Jimmy," Eamon shouted.

"Not so loud," Jimmy shushed.

"It's a woman," Eamon said, in almost a whisper. "I think."

Magillicuddy looked at him blankly. "You *think*?"

"Yeah."

"Who? Mary?"

"No. Not fucking Mary."

"Well, who then?"

"How the hell should I know?" Eamon got up and began to pace and Jimmy sat down.

"You're talking shite," Jimmy said.

"Well," Eamon continued, "it's not really a woman."

"Ah, God. It's not some *Crying Game* thing, is it?"

"I oughta belt you, you know that."

"Eamon, man. What am I supposed to think? It's a woman, *you think*. It's — "

"I'm the one who smashed the Lady."

The words seemed to jump out of Eamon. The confession that he'd swallowed earlier had forced itself up through his esophagus and out his mouth like an unstoppable belch. The effect on Magillicuddy was immediate. He moaned and doubled over as if he'd been struck in the belly.

"Jesus," he wailed. "Mother of God, Eamon. I knew I didn't want to hear this."

"I think — "

"No!" squawked Magillicuddy, and put his hands over his ears. "No! That's it! Not another fucking word. Why me?" he cried. "Why did you have to tell me?" Then he stopped and looked straight at Eamon. "Never mind that. Why the fuck did you do it?"

"That's what she... I mean, this voice keeps asking."

"Ah, Jesus."

"But it doesn't matter why."

"You're right," Magillicuddy said, and began to pace. "I don't want to know. I don't want to know another thing."

"See," Eamon started. "The thing is..."

"Enough!" Jimmy shouted. "No more. Nothing."

Then he stood as still as stone. "Shite," he muttered. "Shite. Shite. Shite. I'm in this." His voice was quick and frightened. He looked around as if he were being watched. "You did it. You told me. I know. I'm fucking in this."

"Jimmy," Eamon said calmly. "Don't you think you're going a bit overboard?"

"Overboard? Overboard, you say? Anybody finds out about this and we'll be fucking crucified."

"That's why nobody's going to find out."

"You're right there." Magillicuddy's voice started to sound weepy. He looked quickly around once more. "I gotta get out of here. I gotta go home." Then he looked at Eamon again. "You stupid twat, you. You stay away from me."

As Jimmy walked away, Eamon felt a definite chill. A cold fear started to flow through his limbs and into his gut. He looked back at the pub then, fingered the throbbing lump over his eye.

The whispering followed Eamon home. Even with his head down and humming, he could hear it. He ran past Mrs. Flannery in the front hall and up the stairs. On the settee he sat with his hands over his ears, but it did no good. The word played itself over and over again: *Why?* He picked up one of the abandoned lagers, now warm, and emptied it in one movement. He did the same with another, to no avail. He closed his eyes. He opened them. He plugged his ears. He unplugged them. Finally he accepted the fact.

"Too much booze. Too much smoke," he said aloud. "I've just pushed myself a little too far. Nothing to worry about."

Then the whispering stopped and everything was fantastically quiet. Except for the sound of his own breathing. As calmly as he could, he leaned forward and picked up the last of the lagers.

"See. Nothing," he mumbled, and lifted the can to his lips. "Just the mind playing tricks, is all."

He leaned back on the settee and sighed. It started again.

"Forget that," Eamon shouted. "This ain't fucking real. It's nothing. It's this," he howled and picked up the joint from two nights before. "Bad weed. So piss off!"

Nothing happened.

"Piss off, I said."

Still nothing.

"Right. That's the way it's going to be, is it?" He stuck the joint in his mouth and lit it. "Fine by me. Let's see if we can't get a whole fucking choir in here."

He sucked the joint. Then again.

"Come on, give us a song," he gasped through the smoke. "An Ave fucking Maria, maybe. That's a nice one."

The whisper changed. The *Why?* ceased. It became something else: his name, soft and gentle. The voice — a mother's voice. His mother's voice.

Eamon dropped the joint and stared into space.

His scream came loud and painful as the spliff burnt through his jeans. He jumped to his feet and grabbed his leg. He doused the settee with warm lager. And the whisper came again, faintly calling his name.

"Enough!" he screamed.

Again and again.

"I've fucking had it! Do you hear me?"

Again.

In one swift movement he grabbed the sledgehammer from the settee and hurled it at the wall. It crashed headfirst through the plaster. Then everything was quiet and he was alone.

He heard the rush of feet on the stairs. A knock at

the door. His name being called.

"Eamon? Eamon? Are you okay?"

Mrs. Flannery slowly opened the door.

"Oh, there you are," she said. "I heard a noise. Are you all right?"

"How'd you get in?"

"I'm sorry, dear." Her voice was mild and soothing. "It was open."

"Did you hear her?"

"Who would that be, then?"

"Her, her. The... woman."

"Well, no." She paused. "Oh, I see. I am sorry. I had no idea." She moved back through the door.

"No, no," he pleaded.

Mrs. Flannery smiled apologetically. "I'm sorry," she whispered. "I didn't mean to barge in."

And she was gone. Eamon could hear her footsteps fade down the stairs. Then he could hear his name again.

He put his hands on his head and slumped back on the settee.

"Please," he begged.

His mother's voice called him. It played in his ears like the ticking of a perpetual clock. He could do nothing to block it out.

He reached for the phone, dialled, and waited.

"Hello?"

"Hugh?"

"Yes. Who is this?" came his brother's tired voice. "Have you any idea the time?"

"It's Eamon."

"I might have guessed," Father Maguire said bitterly. "What do you want?"

"I've got a problem."

"Not surprising."

"I think I've done something terrible."

"Will wonders never cease?" Hugh yawned. "So why are you bothering me?"

"What should I do?"

"Fix it."

And the priest hung up.

Eamon had to hammer on the door a fourth time before the light came on. The curtain in the window was drawn back and Magillicuddy peeked through the glass. A few moments later the door opened to reveal Jimmy in grubby boxers and a Manchester United jersey.

"What are you doing here?" he hissed.

"Nice kit," Eamon sniggered.

"What do you want?" growled Magillicuddy.

Eamon bounced up and down in the cold. He looked cheerful. Almost happy.

"Still got your stuff?" he asked.

"You're out of your fucking head, you are. Coming to my house in the middle of the night for dope."

"James?" a voice came from somewhere in the house. "Who's that, then?"

Jimmy turned around like a frightened rabbit. "No one, Ma. Just a friend."

"Well, tell him to piss off," she shouted back. "It's the middle of the bloody night."

"You heard her," Magillicuddy said. "*Piss off.*"

"That's not the kind of stuff I'm looking for, Jimmy," Eamon said, the smile still on his face. "I want your brick laying gear."

"What?"

"You know," Eamon said. "The stuff you nicked from the building site."

"What do you want that for?"

The smile grew. "I'm going to put the Lady back

together, that's why. I'm going to fix her."

"Go get fucked," Jimmy said with simple slowness.

Eamon stuck a foot in the door and put his face close to Magillicuddy's.

"I know you still got the stuff, Jimmy. And if you don't give it me, I'm going to put my fist straight through to the back of your skull. And if your ma don't like that, I'll do the same for her."

Magillicuddy cringed in the doorway. An involuntary spasm took control of his left cheek.

"It's around back in the shed."

"Good job, son," Eamon said, and gave the quivering cheek a gentle slap.

The first thing Eamon did was pile the rubble according to size. It took him a while to collect the smaller pieces and he was fairly certain some had already been pocketed. The larger fragments he rolled into place, wanting to save his energy for the task ahead. Then he mixed the mortar in a tin bucket. Never having practiced the art of masonry, he was unsure of the proper recipe. So he added small amounts of water from Magillicuddy's jerry can until he had a dark grey sludge the consistency of wet sand. Then he looked at the piles. He would have to work in reverse. When he'd taken her apart he'd started with the head. Now it was to be feet up.

He slapped the mortar onto the broken ankles still set on the pedestal, then searched for the brief calves which disappeared into the solid alabaster hem of the robe. The weight of the stone took his breath away, and he had to bend deep at the knees to lift it from the ground. The mortar hissed as the fragment settled. Without hesitating, Eamon spread another layer of mortar. The next section, which took in from just below the knees to above the waist, was in three long slices. He slathered mortar along their edges, then, after readying himself as he'd seen weightlifters do on the telly, put them into position in quick, successive movements. Then he wrapped his arms tightly around the hips. Unsure of how long it would take to set, he slowly counted out ten minutes, then stepped back.

The torso was in two segments. The sledgehammer had severed it with almost surgical precision just below the breasts. Eamon spread the last of the mortar across the fractured hips, then turned his attention to the midriff. His face and arms grew slick with sweat as he struggled to hoist up the rubble. He stopped and leaned against the low grotto wall, readjusting his grip, before executing a jerk that landed the belly solidly into place. Then he sat down on the wet grass and lit a cigarette. His lungs burned with the same intensity as his fag-ember, but the discomfort couldn't keep the smile from his face as he looked up at the figure which had begun to form before him. Then, just as he was about to apply the trowel to the next portion, a light came on in the rectory. He fell to the ground and froze, as his brother's shadow approached the window.

"Shite," Eamon said, under his breath. "Piss off."

The priest, as if he'd heard him, moved away from the window and the light went out. Eamon lay motionless for a further five minutes to make certain the light did not come on again. Then he got back to his feet, found the trowel, and plastered the flat surface of the belly.

Eamon found the bosom far more difficult than the belly. The added weight of the breasts pulled hard on his shoulders, and stretched the muscles in his back almost to the point of snapping. The veins in his neck bulged; his throat constricted. He had to stand on the grotto wall to reach the next level of the statue. She hadn't seemed so big when he'd smashed her to the ground.

When his breath finally returned, he looked again to the pile of rubble. Only the head was recognizable. The arms were nowhere to be found.

"You've got to be joking," Eamon muttered.

He shrugged, picked up the head and slathered a healthy dollop of mortar across the base of the throat. The excess he wiped onto the filthy leg of his jeans. Then he held the head between his hands — a palm covering each ear — and slowly lowered it onto the broken neck. The jagged edges matched exactly, and the halo offered a perfect pressure point that Eamon used to force the fractured contours together.

A broad smile creased his face. He tweaked the statue's nose and jumped down. Then he turned his attention to the small pile of shattered debris. He picked through the wreckage and set aside edge pieces, as if he were doing a jigsaw puzzle. Then he found two fingers: index and middle, attached at their base. He turned them over in his hand.

From behind him came a short chuckling sound, soft and low. Almost like a snigger, but whispered. He turned around to see the statue begin to shift. The head tilted to the left, then began to nod.

HOLLYWOOD,
HERE WE COME

The door was unlocked and Gladys walked in. It was that easy. She'd expected somebody to be standing guard, one of those men with the walkie-talkie headsets or maybe even a police officer, but there was no one. She just turned the metal handle, opened the thin aluminum door and climbed the three steps into warmth. Perhaps she wouldn't need the gun after all; perhaps he would understand.

She was taken by the interior of the recreational vehicle. That's what they called them nowadays, recreational vehicles, RV's. When she and Bert had looked at one a few years back they called them Winnebagos, but not anymore. Even so, the one they looked at — a cottage on wheels, the dealer said — was nothing compared to this. The carpet felt three feet thick, its pile discernible through the soles of her boots. And the panelling looked as if it were real oak, so much nicer than the veneered pressboard in her living room. Even the sink and fixtures shone like polished sterling. I could live in this, Gladys thought, I really could.

A cough interrupted her reverie and she turned.

There he was. Gladys almost hiccuped with excitement and for a moment felt faint. Jake Shackles, né Yakov Shalinsky. Gladys knew everything about him, from his impoverished childhood in the Brighton Beach section of Brooklyn to his turbulent stint at the Actors' Studio; from his genius for villainy in so many RKO westerns to his, in her opinion, underrated work in those low-budget slasher films of the late-seventies. As a teenager she used to drink up every word about him, and there were many, in *Silver Screen* and *Photoplay*. And even now she would scour the pages of *People* and *Us* for mention of him, a much rarer occurrence.

He looked older than he had the last time Gladys had seen him on screen, as the at-first kindly farmer who turned out to be the psychopathic scythe-killer in *Grim Reaper*. He wasn't as tall as she imagined and his shoulders bore a greater hunch. His steely-grey hair was still steely-grey, but somewhat thinner than it looked on film. The one thing that hadn't changed, that had remained the same since his face first shone through celluloid, was the creases that stretched from the corners of his soft blue eyes; those rugged folds of flesh bracketed his every emotion: happy, sad, angry, maniacal. And, of course, the slight bend on the bridge of his nose, which he had broken at the age of eleven falling from the stoop of his parents' Neptune Avenue tenement.

The incongruities made no difference to Gladys, though. What mattered was that he was there. Jake Shackles was there in Denniter, Ontario, a mere flyspeck on the road map of the province. He was there in his RV, sitting behind a table that Gladys thought must be real marble, not just painted Formica, drinking coffee from a black mug with his name stencilled across it in big white letters. And even more thrilling was the fact that she was there too.

"Mr Shackles," Gladys said, taking a step toward him. "Jake...Yakov."

He straightened slightly in his seat and smiled, those famous crow's feet deepening with his grin. "I think, my dear," he said, in the cavernous, rough voice that had set countless busty coeds to screaming and legions of anaemic homesteaders to quaking, "you have made a wrong turn."

"Oh, no," Gladys twittered, unable to keep the school-girlish blush from her cheeks. "No, I'm supposed to be here."

She could feel the weight of Bert's target pistol in her coat pocket. *Silly to have brought it,* she thought, *he seems such a gentleman.* My dear. How could he not understand?

This is what it has come to, all that potential and this is where I am, Artie Phritter thought. The continuous wheeze of the firehoses filled his ears as he watched the white mucous spew forth from their nozzles. Looks more like yogurt than snow, someone behind him had said. The white goop that drifted through the air and landed, with the delicacy of vomit, on the sloping porch roof and brown grass reminded Artie of whipped topping rather than yogurt. It had the same swirl to it as the picture on the plastic tubs he'd seen in the grocery store. No doubt it had been *whipped up* by some effects-dingbat who'd been given one too many chemistry sets as a child. Earlier he'd mustered enough interest to ask one of the technicians what the gunk was made of. He hadn't been surprised when he'd found out the main ingredient was animal fat; the stuff smelled like rotting corpses.

All around him was a bustle with techs and PAs and sundry other peons hurrying to dress the set. A sixteen-day shoot and already they were two days behind. The Ghost of Christmas Past, who'd been flying up from New York, got caught by Canada Customs carrying the wrong kind of snow. Artie had tried to make light of it with the producer, muttering something about *A White Christmas*. Under normal circumstances — normal meaning if Artie'd had other scenes ready to shoot — he was sure the producer would have seen the humour. As it was, they canned the apparition from the Empire State, scampered about to find one in Toronto, and lost two days and several thousand dollars in the process.

What a joke, Artie thought as he watched the viscous snow slop from the porch roof. A modern day re-telling of the Dickens' classic, exactly two hours from fade-in to fade-out after the commercials had been slotted. What was the point? They should have left well enough alone after Simms. Even that Bill Murray vehicle — which Artie knew he could have done a better job with — paled by comparison. And now this tripe. Without question it was a waste of his talent. He'd been to UCLA with Coppola, for God's sake, and his student offerings had far outshone those of that Book-of-the-Month-Club plunderer. Even people who weren't his friends said so. And hadn't his first picture made waves on the art house circuit? So what if you never saw the actors' faces; so what if there was no discernible plot or structure? It was free-form, revolutionary. It was the sixties. And so what if he had made a few wrong turns in the seventies rather than grab every pot-boiler on the bestseller list? *I stuck to my principles*, Artie thought, *and this is what I get? Puerile movie-of-the-week dross?* And his agent had to fight tooth and nail for this crud because the bloody network didn't even know who he was.

"They'll be ready in five minutes, Artie. Maybe we'd better run through this."

Artie looked into the acne-blistered face of his AD. The kid was probably twenty-five and Artie couldn't stand him. Someone's nephew, more than likely. His manner was as greasy as his skin and he was altogether too familiar. Artie refused to remember his name.

"Okay," Artie said. "Talk."

As the kid dribbled out his opinion — wanting to make full use of the crane, à la Spielberg — Artie sat with his fingertips pressed together and his eyes closed. No doubt the little twerp thought he was contemplating the genius of his *mise en scène*. Instead, Artie was re-examining his lot, revelling in his pathetic circumstance. There was a point, before he'd signed onto the project, when he'd relished the thought of making the picture. The script had always been, and always would be, crap. But he was little concerned with quality. His hopes, then, had been pinned on the inevitability of an on-set dalliance. Maybe a cute AD or story editor he could promise advancement to, or possibly even a roustabout with the leading lady. As it turned out, every member of the crew, both male and female, seemed to be skimmed from the same gene pool as the unctuous twit beside him. And the principals were anything but A-list, in looks and talent. They'd even saddled him with that dinosaur Jake Shackles. When he'd met with the network executives in New York, they had gushed at signing the actor. A legend, the one with the long blonde hair and supple legs had said. *A legend, indeed*, Artie thought, *like the Loch Ness Monster*. The old fart only had two expressions, both of them psychotic. But the woman had been stunning and Artie would have agreed with anything she said for the opportunity to lick the inside of her thigh. Which he never got.

The spotty AD droned on, but Artie ignored him. He

was still thinking about Shackles. Even that cardboard Hollywood cast-off was getting some. Sure, the woman he saw creeping into his trailer was on the dumpy side, and looked old enough to be Artie's mother, but what could you expect at Shackles' age? The old prick was lucky anyone under sixty even recognized his craggy face.

"So, what do you think, Artie?" the kid said.

"I think you should call me Mr. Phritter," Artie replied, and added, "You little shit," in his head. The firehoses were still spitting their sludge over the set: five minutes in movie time, an hour in the real world. Artie pushed himself out of the director's chair. *Will it ever end?* he wondered.

The *Denniter Bugle* had trumpeted the news. Three-inch headlines stretched across the front page. The last time the paper had used letters that size was to announce the end of the Second World War and even then it had done so a week late. Still, the lavish use of ink seemed appropriate, considering it heralded what was the most significant dispatch for the town since the cessation of hostilities. The headline read: "Hollywood Here We Come." In actual fact, the town was going nowhere, it was Hollywood that was coming to Denniter.

Gladys Pollip almost melted when she read the story. Sitting at her kitchen table, with her sugar-coated Shredded Wheat and Red Rose Tea, the television tuned to *Rosie O'Donnell*, she felt the spark of something she thought had died long ago. It was like a tingling at first, then a pain, then a great shifting bubble; it lingered in the area just above her navel. Ordinarily, she would have swallowed some Alka-Seltzer in hopes of burping it away. But re-reading the front page of the *Bugle*, Gladys knew that her symptoms had nothing to do with indigestion. Rather, it was a sensation that had been absent for so long she'd almost forgotten it had ever existed. She slipped a hand under her nightgown and ran her fingers across the loosening flesh beneath her breasts. It was there, discernible to the touch. Gladys tried to remember the last time she'd been visited by this impression. It was somewhere deep in the past. She closed her eyes, rubbed her tummy, and let the years fall away. So far back. Before Bert or after? she wondered. Then she found it. She stopped rubbing and smiled. Yes, just before Bert; right before their wedding. The very day, in fact. She was at her parents' house, sitting in their bedroom in front of her mother's vanity, the maid of honour — Joan-Lee Sweeney — had just set the veil on her head and when Gladys looked into the mirror she had felt it. And thinking about it now, she knew what it was. That discomfort in her midsection, that belonged to no single organ and yet to all of them, had nothing to do with her gastric juices. It had to do with hope.

Gladys glanced through the article again. The big American TV network's Christmas special, *Humbug*, would be filming in Denniter for two days at the end of October. Two crowd scenes, Christmas Eve and Christmas morning, and all Denniterians were encouraged to join. Everyone was asked to wear their normal winter clothing and invited to bring their pets — if well behaved. They would be paid, as well. Five dollars an hour. The money made no difference to Gladys. She would have done it for free.

At the bottom of the page were photographs of the stars. Gladys didn't recognize the actor playing Cratchit, but Amanda Glenn was to portray his wife. Gladys knew her. She had been in that wonderful sitcom a few years back, about the single mom who suffered no end of humourous misfortune at the hands of her twin toddlers. Unfortunately, the show didn't last long. Then there was that terrible bit of scandal after she had had her breasts enlarged and did the pictorial in that girlie magazine. They had made it all into a movie-of-the-week, *Amanda Glenn, Her Story*. Amanda Glenn had played herself.

But even better than Amanda Glenn, though she was exciting, was Jake Shackles as Ebeneezer Scrooge. Gladys swooned slightly at his picture. When she was a teenager and all the other girls hugged their pillows and dreamed of James Dean, Marlon Brando and Montgomery Clift, Gladys had clutched hers and dreamed of Shackles. And unlike those other leading men, who either died young or grew old and bloated, her Jake had aged with grace and dignity, even if his career had not.

Gladys didn't realize she was crying until a tear fell onto the corner of Jake Shackles' picture. The ink began to run before she could blot away the wetness. Luckily only his shoulder smudged. After she dried her eyes, Gladys used the edge of the table to carefully tear his photo from the paper. She put it into the pocket of her housecoat, then got up and went to the phone. She wanted to call Bert at work and tell him the news.

Rosabelle Fouschnicki wanted nothing more than to smoke a peaceful cigarette. To be out of this crummy little community hall with its paint-by-number landscapes, dusty trophy cases, tuneless piano and broken heating. Yesterday had almost killed her. It seemed as if the entire town had shown up and not one of them had been an extra before. They'd been harder to control than a kindergarten class. They huddled about in little groups and chatted as if it were a potluck dinner. Potluck is what they were all right, as far as

Rosabelle was concerned. She had signed them all up, even though she knew she shouldn't have and sent them out to the set. Let them worry about it, she'd decided. And worry they did. Adam Bickerstaff, the odious little AD, had tracked her down and thrown a fit. "Too many," he screamed. "We have too many." Then he told Rosabelle that if she couldn't handle the job he would gladly find another agency that could. It was a bluff, she knew, but for the sake of future contracts she told him she would weed out some for the second day. The process was easy enough: those who wore the same clothes were gone; those who didn't pay her the reverence she felt she was due were gone; those who had red hair, a colour she despised, were gone.

It helped that she didn't like people. It made it easier to be cruel. And because Rosabelle detested others so much, she rarely had to raise her voice against them. A cold stare and a deadly calm tone were more than sufficient to dispatch any grievant. She employed the same method with amourous drunks, weeping old ladies and frightened children. And she relished the thought of using it on the backwoods yokels of Denniter.

She had already managed to cull the herd of townies by a third. Some she cut loose face to face with lines like: "the director asked specifically *not* to have you back," and "with a look like that you were lucky to have got on-set at all." Others drifted away before they even reached her, not wanting to face the same humiliation dealt to their neighbours. For the most part, the dismissals went without incident. A few rude remarks were made, but they had been delivered with feeble indignation. There was nothing that could be said that Rosabelle hadn't heard before.

Only one person caused her a problem. Only one person forced Rosabelle into raising her voice. An older woman in a long, purple puffy coat, with a bulky, knitted toque a shade or two darker. Her hands were tucked into a rabbit-fur muff. To look at her, bundled up as she was, the woman could have been anywhere between forty-five and sixty. Rosabelle guessed she tended toward the latter. The woman stood there, looking down at her with a grin so wide it seemed her face might split.

"I'm back," she said, in a thin, piping voice.

"That coat," Rosabelle said, already having made her decision, "were you wearing it yesterday?"

"Yes."

"Then I'm afraid we can't use you."

"But..." The word sounded more like a belch. Rosabelle ignored the eructation and turned back to her list. But the woman did not move. Rosabelle waited, her pen hovering above the paper. Still the woman stood. Fine, Rosabelle thought, if that's what it's going to take. She let the comforting callousness settle into her features, a perfect countenance of malice. Then she looked again at the woman.

"Well?"

"But I only have one coat."

"Your wardrobe is no concern of mine."

"But it doesn't make any sense."

"And what would you know about sense?" Rosabelle felt good, strong. She could see the wetness pooling in the corners of the woman's eyes.

"Why would a person wear one coat one day," the woman said, her voice beginning to choke, "and a different one the next?"

"Look," Rosabelle hissed — she was enjoying herself and would have revelled in carrying on the degradation, but they would be calling the extras to set any minute. "If I say you're out, you're out. Simple as that. Now get lost."

This is where the woman should have crumbled.

Broken like many had before her. But she did nothing of the sort. Rather, the moisture in her eyes evaporated like spit on an iron and her wanness hardened. The airy mass of her jacket seemed to become her body itself, making the woman frighteningly large. She removed her hands from the muff and placed them flat on the table, then leaned in close. The humidity of her breath startled Rosabelle.

"You listen to me, you little witch," the woman snarled. "You are not going to stop me from doing this."

Rosabelle was silent. The woman hadn't uttered a single profanity and yet her tone bespoke every curse imaginable. It was as if she had reached out and slapped her. Rosabelle could feel the sting. And for the life of her she could not find a rebuke. It was as if, like a chalkboard, her mind had been wiped clean. The woman looked down at her, a small light of victory creeping into her eyes. And then it came. Arriving in an angry rush and with such a hollering force that one might have thought her lungs had the capacity of an airship.

"You listen to me, you goddamn cow!" Rosabelle screamed. "You're out. Do you hear me? Out! Now piss off before I call security and have them throw you out!"

Gunslinger, Ride On, RKO Pictures, 1952: The small California gold rush town of Hope has fallen under the control of a menacing band of desperadoes led by the one-eyed, one-armed outlaw, Lefty Diablo. Lefty and his gang of whiskey-drinking, tobacco-chewing ruffians run rampant through Hope, defiling the wives of innocent farmers, looting the stock of honest merchants, jumping the claims of hard-working prospectors. All live in fear. All, that is, except Melody Sweete, daughter of Jonah, proprietor of the Last Chance Saloon and Inn. Once a reputable establishment, the Last Chance, like everything else in Hope, has been taken over by the evil Lefty and his boys. They have ensconced themselves in its rooms and forced the weaker women of the town into prostitution, to serve themselves and the weaker men. But not Melody. She has remained steadfast against the threat of harlotry, as well as the advances of the nefarious Lefty. The last bastion of morality in Hope, Melody faces many dangers and is on the verge of being violated by one of Lefty's henchmen, a half-breed with an immense scar running the length of his face, when she is saved by a quiet stranger. The newcomer rescues Melody's virtue and deals a severe beating to the snivelling half-breed. There is an undeniable attraction between sweet Melody Sweete and the stranger. But the quiet man is carrying many burdens, there is a darkness in his heart that keeps him from intimacy. His lame horse waylays him in Hope, but he refuses the entreaties of Melody and Jonah to help rid the town of Lefty and his gang. Refuses, that is, until Lefty and three of his flunkies, the scarred half-breed among them, track him down outside the livery stable. It is here, as they stare each other down, that the town drunk, formerly Hope's respected doctor, recognizes the stranger from years before in Deadwood. A gunslinger, he was, a born killer. The bullets fly. When the smoke settles, Lefty and his minions lay dead in the dirt. The gunslinger is wounded and, with his head in Melody's lap, loses consciousness. The doctor, sober now, nurses him to health, telling him that his secret is out. The stranger frets that his past has come back to haunt him. The town, the doctor says, thinks otherwise. But the gunslinger knows better. It is time for him to ride on. The final scene: Melody and the stranger standing out front of Jonah's saloon, now re-named the Faithful. A tear runs down Melody's cheek.

The stranger wipes it away. He promises to return, but she knows he never will. He mounts his horse. As the music swells, the gunslinger rides out of Hope. He does not look back.

It was Gladys' favourite film and the only western in which Jake Shackles portrayed the hero. It had been a box-office failure, even with Gladys seeing it eight times. As a teen, she used to imagine she was Melody, and would walk around the house with the straight-backed pride Myrna Royal had affected in the role of the pure Miss Sweete. But the part of the movie Gladys had liked best was when Jake Shackles swooped out of the shadows, the righteous avenger. She would play the scene out before the floor length mirror in her bedroom. A flannel nightgown with a big wool scarf tied around the waist served as her pioneer-girl's frock. She would twist her face into paroxysms of shock and horror as the half-breed advanced toward her, intent on defilement. Sometimes she would alter the features of her assailant: the principal of her high school, the clerk at the postoffice who always smelled of gin, once, before she had started going steady with him, she even imagined it to be Bert. Then there would be a sound, just behind her to the right, behind the closet door, and her eyes would widen with a new terror. But it was not another attacker. No, it was Jake Shackles, bursting into her bedroom and delivering her from danger. The difference in Gladys' rendering of the story was that Jake, her handsome stranger, did not act cold and standoffish afterward, rather he threw her onto the bed and passionately kissed her; or more correctly, Gladys embraced her pillow and buried her face into its stuffing.

She felt funny telling him all this, letting him into her secret world of so long ago. But why not? Gladys thought. After all, he was there, too. In a way, at least. She wished he could have seen her then. So slim, so beautiful. Her legs had been long and athletic; dancer's legs, her mother had called them. And her hair was like cornsilk. All in all, her body had been quite fetching, her buttocks pleasantly round, her breasts firm and alert. Her face was as smooth as soap, not a single blemish. Gladys wished so much it had been that version of her, held coquettishly within the cinched nightgown, that stood before Jake Shackles, not this one in the bulky mauve jacket, ratty toque and heavy boots.

"You were really lovely in that," she gushed. "The studio should have let you play the good guy more often. You were so powerful."

"Why, thank you, sweet lady," Jake Shackles said. He was still sitting behind the table, still holding his coffee mug. "I'm afraid, though, I don't remember much of that picture. I was drinking a great deal back then."

The poor soul, Gladys thought. It was true, he did have some rough times in the early fifties. There were his two failed marriages, and the rumours about he and Myrna Royal and her being in the family way. All of it was nonsense, of course. Lies spread by muckrakers who were jealous of his obvious talent. Anyone could see that *Gunslinger, Ride On* should have made Jake Shackles a star. It had been sabotage, pure and simple, Gladys decided.

"Well," Shackles said, sliding from behind the table, "this has been lovely...uh?"

"Gladys."

"Yes. Gladys. As I said, this has been lovely, but I really must get to the set."

"No," Gladys said, a bit too loudly. And she could feel the weight again in her pocket. "No. You needn't go yet." She began to blush. "I mean, I'm sure they'll send someone when they're ready for you."

She hadn't thought about that.

Bickerstaff, that was the little puke's name. Adam Bickerstaff. It just leapt into Artie's mind, and before he could expunge it again, it leapt from his mouth.

"Yes, Artie?"

"What?"

"You called me, Artie."

"No I didn't. Go away."

What was with that kid? He was everywhere. Artie Phritter had snuck from the set and down a side street to the craft-services truck for the express purpose of escaping the little runt and with one slip of the tongue, there he was, a persistent gnat, buzzing in his ear. Artie made a note to talk to his agent. On the next picture he would demand the right to pick his own crew: cinematographer, art director, and AD. And the bloody location scout, too, thought Artie. No more of this hundred-miles-from-nowhere crap. From now on he would only shoot in big cities. Big cities with disco-lighted night clubs and smoky bars and fine restaurants and women, good-looking leggy young women he could dazzle with his charm and tales of Hollywood — or at least pay for and charge it to the cost of production.

He took a Styrofoam bowl and plastic spoon from the slack-jawed craft-services girl and headed back toward the set. The first mouthful of the slop made him gag. Noodles and tofu smothered in a thick red sauce. He dropped it into a garbage pail beside the truck. Whatever happened to the good food, the real food? The fresh shrimp, the filet mignon, the braised chicken? Hell, Liz and Dick had had chili con carné flown in all the way from Monterey. Another note: next time he would have final say on the food, as well.

Next time. Who was he trying to kid? Next time would be the same as this, if he were lucky. More than likely he'd be back shooting pirouetting distended veins for hemorrhoidal cream commercials. Which is exactly what he had been doing before he signed onto this gig. Delivered from proctol hell into low-grade purgatory. And with no one to bang.

It hadn't always been that way. On his first film, his underground hit *Scatolingus* — half a cup of Warhol, a tablespoon of Buster Keaton with just a pinch of Man Ray, according to the *Village Voice* — he'd had more sex than he could handle. Even during the disastrous vortex that was the seventies, with *Witch Hunt*, *Mile Wide* and that catastrophic Civil War epic, *Run Rebel, Run*, he'd been able to keep his wick dipped. There was always a young actress who needed her talent confirmed. Where were they now? *One thing is for certain*, Artie thought, *they're not on the set of Humbug.* The only female working on the picture even worth looking at was that nipped-and-tucked sitcom failure, Amanda Glenn. And she wouldn't let anyone get within three feet of her for fear her silicone implants might pop.

"Artie. *Artie?*"

It was the gnat again, buzz-buzzing. Artie wished he had a rolled-up newspaper to swat him with. "What?"

"We're ready, Artie."

"Well," Artie said with simple slowness, as close to the kid's ravaged complexion as he dared get, "then let's get it over with, shall we."

Christ, he missed the old days.

The Denniter Town Council had printed up flyers to announce the film's arrival. The pictures of the actors from the *Bugle* had been blown up and arranged in a pyramid, with Jake Shackles at the top. Information for those who wanted to take part was also included. "See you in the movies" was written along the bottom in big, bold letters surrounded by hand-drawn stars.

Gladys Pollip stood before the "Community News" bulletin board at the back of the A&P and stared at the flyer. She could feel the shifting bubble again. Her mind was made up: no matter what Bert said, she was going down to the community hall next Thursday morning. She would leave before he got up for work, that way he would have no say in the matter. He was just being stupid, anyhow. Telling her there was no way a wife of his was going to prance about like a fool with all those Hollywood dope-fiends and perverts. He never did like Jake Shackles.

"So?" a voice behind her said. "What do you think?"

It was Jeanie Flowers, her neighbour from across the road. Jeanie had a loaf of Wonder Bread and a carton of whole milk in her arms.

"You gonna go down, or what?" she asked.

"Are you?"

"Frank doesn't want me to."

"Neither does Bert," Gladys said. She looked back to the flyer, to the picture of Jake Shackles. "But I'm going anyhow."

"Good for you," Jeanie said, shifting her load. "I thought about it, but I'm going to look after the babies, instead. So the kids can go."

Jeanie's children were the same age as Gladys'. But unlike Gladys', they had remained in Denniter and started families of their own. The Pollip children, Matt and Judy, had moved down to Toronto and rarely called their mother. This was not a fact that Gladys found terribly upsetting.

"Ladies," another voice said.

Myn Crawley pushed her shopping cart between Jeanie and Gladys. It was loaded to overflowing with brand names, all bought without the aid of a single coupon. Gladys did not like Myn. Not her frosted hair, her lined lips, nor her aerobicized body. She dressed too much like a daughter, rather than a mother.

"I think it's just fantastic," Myn went on. "I can't wait to see Amanda Glenn. I want to ask her about her boobs."

"A little inappropriate, Myn, don't you think?" Jeanie said, raising her eyebrows to Gladys.

"Oh, I won't be crude. Besides, I expect I'll be spending quite some time with her."

"How do you figure?" Gladys asked.

Myn Crawley sighed and shook her head. The way she made people feel that she was suffering their presence irked Gladys. Mostly because it always affected her in the exact way Myn intended, leaving her with a sense of inferiority.

"Picasso," Myn said, "of course."

"Of course," Jeanie echoed, nodding sagely.

Picasso, the Crawley's basset hound, was the pride of Myn's life. Two years earlier, the dog had appeared sad-eyed and lazy on a billboard for a new brand of kibble. Not the most glowing endorsement for a product that expounded a healthy diet for frisky canines. Nevertheless, ever since, Myn Crawley had squired the pooch around town as if it were Benji himself.

"I have no doubt that they will want him for close-ups. Maybe even work him into the story somehow." Myn pulled on her fur-lined leather gloves. "He has an agent, you know. Which reminds me, I have to give him a call, so I'm afraid I can't stay and chat."

Gladys and Jeanie watched her as she pushed her cart through the automatic doors and out into the parking lot. Then laughed when one of the bags split as she hoisted it into the trunk of her European car.

The piss gathered itself in a small pool beside Rosabelle Fouschnicki's right boot. The day felt as if it would never end and she still hadn't had her cigarette. With only six people left in line, the dog lady had shown up, pushing her way straight to the front and throwing an elbow into the ribs of the rheumy-eyed geezer who Rosabelle had just decided could stay. And then the dog, some genetic mishap from a puppy mill, lifted its leg and pissed.

"I'm sorry I'm late," the dog lady said, flicking her brittle permed hair loose from her collar, "but Picasso was having some tummy troubles."

"He'll be having some ass troubles after I stick my boot up his rear," Rosabelle growled.

"I beg your pardon?"

Rosabelle had seen this kind of woman before. There was at least one on every shoot. Demanding, oblivious, ignorant and woefully out-of-date in the fashion department: a real Joan Crawford. It was usually a kid they were parading around, though, not a filthy mutt. Rosabelle would have liked nothing more than to knock the pegs from under the dog lady and her drooling hound; to vitiate her right here, in the middle of the community hall, before all those who had to suffer her existence daily. Rosabelle wanted to be the deliverer of the yokels; wanted to slay for them, with her vitriol, the dragon dog lady. But she couldn't. That prick Bickerstaff wouldn't let her. He'd been quite clear about it the night before when he threw his tantrum. "I don't care what you do with the rest of them," he'd bleated, "but the dog stays. Artie wants it for the final shot." Rosabelle took a deep breath and slowly stood.

"Right," she hissed. "The rest of you, you're gone. That means you, too, old man." Then she looked into the smiling, plucked and pancaked face of the dog lady and added, "You can thank Queenie here for missing out." And as she turned away from the table, Rosabelle carefully aimed the toe of her boot at the dog's front paw and stepped down hard.

The words fell like water from Gladys' lips. It was the knock on the door that did it. Just after she'd realized they would send someone to get him, she'd engaged the lock. Then came knuckles wrapping on the flimsy metal. A thin voice, like a teenaged boy heading into puberty, calling for Mr. Shackles. It frightened her. And she gushed like a broken faucet.

"I don't love my husband. I don't think I ever did. Not even when I married him. I felt something, I'm sure. But not love. He's a horrible man. Horrible. He treats me bad. Talks down to me. Belittles me. I am not a child. I deserve respect. But does Bert respect me? Not on your life. He treats me like I'm an object. A thing he owns. Like a fishing pole or work bench. Property. A thing he can roll on top of every Wednesday night when he gets home from hockey. Five minutes of groaning. His fat, hairy belly pushing against me, soaking through my night gown, he sweats so much. I lie there and hope his heart gives out. He doesn't even shower after the game. Comes home stinking of BO and beer. It's disgusting. He's a pig.

"The kids are the same. As ungrateful as their father. They worked me like a mule. Then they turn around and treat me like a I'm halfwit. Don't you think I wanted to get out of this hole of a town? Don't you think I wanted something more than this? How do they think they got their chance? It was me. I'm the one who had to squeeze the dimes out of their father so they could go away to school. I'm the one that had to take the job at the Valu-Mart so they could have the nice clothes. Had to go down there and wear that ridiculous smock and listen to the high school girls I worked with laugh behind my back. Me. I'm the one that had to go without so they could go with.

"Well, screw them all. That's right, I said screw them. It's time for me now. Let's see how they manage on their own. If they can manage. I doubt it. And I don't care. They're not going to have Mother around to wipe their feet on anymore. No, sir. It's my turn. It's Gladys' turn."

Her mouth was dry. Sawdust. It was as if all the moisture had been wrung from her body. And no tears. It felt strange. Good, but strange. She looked at Jake Shackles. Those eyes. She could see in them that he understood. The way the creases folded in on themselves with compassion. This was right. As he took a step toward her, Gladys felt seventeen again. Her bulky winter coat felt like a night gown.

He'd been in Mexico with Peckinpah. Peckinpah, Coburn, Kristofferson and Artie Phritter. He wasn't even working on the film, just hanging out with Sam. Dylan was there, too. Squirrelly little monkey of a man, he was. He'd only signed on to do the soundtrack, but once Sam got a look at him, that was it. He had no choice but to be in the picture. Peckinpah scared him into doing it. The five of them and the tequila, the peyote, the cocaine, the women. Lovely little señoritas with smooth skin, big eyes and no English. They were fourteen if they were a day, Artie thought.

The festering snow was still being sprayed. The firehoses had been abandoned for insecticide canisters strapped to the technicians' backs. The twit, Bickerstaff, was directing the assault, making certain every branch of every tree that might make it into the shot was coated with the glutinous crap. "Make it real," he kept chirping. "Make it real."

Real, Phritter thought. Real was burying chickens up to their necks, then squirting lighter fluid into their eyes so they wouldn't fall asleep before the explosive charges strapped beneath their beaks had a chance to go off. That was real. Peckinpah was a god. A madman, yes, but still a god. He would have killed himself before working on a joke like this. Which is pretty much what he did in the end, anyway. So Sam was dead. And Coburn was sober. Kristofferson had found God, and Dylan — well, Dylan was so screwed up he might as well have been dead, too. And Artie Phritter?

Artie shook his head. He'd had enough.

"Hey, kid," he shouted. "You, gnat."

Bickerstaff poked his head up on the far side of the set. Artie could swear he saw his ears prick. Then he came loping through the sludge like a big, stupid dog.

"You want me, Artie?"

"Yeah. Go get Shackles so we can do this thing."

Bickerstaff turned and snapped his fingers at a young woman in a headset, with a clipboard and a parka that was suited for the Arctic.

"No," Artie said. "Not her. I want *you* to get Shackles."

"Me? But Artie, I'm the—"

"What are you, deaf?" Artie said, calmly. "You."

The kid turned and started to mope off the set. And for the first time that day, for the first time the entire shoot, Artie felt good. The dismay and hurt in his AD's eyes gave him a warm feeling in his belly, like Bourbon.

Gladys Pollip couldn't believe that Jake Shackles had touched her. The director, or at least she assumed it was the director, was so angry with her she'd been close to tears. The scene had been explained to them so many times it felt like they'd already done it. It was Christmas Eve, the main street was crowded with last minute shoppers, Scrooge was leaving his office. Gladys was amazed at how they'd transformed Denniter into an identical small American town. New signs were nailed above all the shops, and the red

Canada Post boxes had been replaced by their blue American cousins. Everything was exactly the same but completely different. Denniter, Ontario had become New London, Nebraska right before her eyes. It was fantastic. Then someone yelled, then someone else, and all of a sudden he was there. Jake Shackles standing on the steps of what used to be the Century 21 office but was now the S&M Savings & Loan. He turned then, descended the steps and started down the sidewalk toward her. Just as he was about to pass her, Gladys extended her hand. She was about to say how wonderful she thought he was when:

"Cut!" The voice seemed as if it were coming from everywhere. "What the hell do you think you're doing?"

What was she, stupid? the director had screamed. Did she not understand the instructions? Who was she that she thought she could ruin a scene in *his* film? If she did it again he would make sure that not only would she not be in frame, she wouldn't even be on the bloody set. He hollered so close to her face that she could smell the sourness of his breath. Then Jake Shackles put his hand on her shoulder. And when she turned round to look into that face she'd dreamed of for so many years, it was smiling the sweetest, kindest smile she'd ever seen.

"Don't worry about it, my dear," Shackles said, giving a squeeze. "That one didn't feel right to me, anyway."

My God, Gladys thought, *he's perfect.*

Maybe she'd go to Aruba. Or the Bahamas, or Antigua. One of those squalid little Caribbean isles where she could flash American money and her pale flabby skin at the ebony natives on the beach. Then she would bring one of them back to her hotel room, use him and throw him away like the complimentary soap. The thought of it warmed Rosabelle Fouschnicki as she smoked her long-awaited cigarette on the metal fire escape outside the community hall. With winter coming on a vacation was just what she needed, she told herself. She had hoarded away enough for at least a month in the sun; two, if she found a cheap resort. She could leave tomorrow if she wanted. All that was left of this shoot was to sign the vouchers and hand out the cash. The accounts department back at the agency could worry about the rest. As far as Rosabelle was concerned, she was finished.

She pulled out another cigarette and lit it off the stub of her first. It tasted better than mother's milk. She could feel a headache coming on and tried to decide whether to take Tylenol 3 or Seconal to curtail its arrival. She went with the latter, its opiate qualities winning out. The scene with the dog lady had nettled her. Not because she had to bite her tongue, the painful yelp of the dog had assuaged that, rather because it had prompted her to dismiss the others en masse. Except for the old man, Rosabelle knew she would have rejected the rest anyway, but the dog lady had robbed her of the satisfaction of doing it on an individual basis. "I should quit," she said to herself, as she leaned back against the fire door, "Quit and go live in the West Indies. Work in a hotel." But then she figured that tourist people were probably even worse than the regular everyday fare. So, she took another long drag of her cigarette and looked out across the parking lot, to the edge of the playing field where the equipment trucks and motor homes were parked. She recognized the figure in the big purple coat shuffling through the mud at the edge of the asphalt. It stopped a moment, peered down the line of tractor-trailers, then moved on again. Just outside the wardrobe truck it paused again, before making directly for Jake Shackles' trailer.

"Christ," Rosabelle muttered. "It's amazing what some people will do to get into the movies."

"Can you believe it?" Gladys said, holding her hand out. The target pistol was lying in her palm, looking more like a children's toy than a lethal weapon. "I don't even know why I brought it. I don't know what I was thinking. Nuts, isn't it?"

Jake Shackles was standing in the middle of what the Winnebago salesman would have called the *family room*. He seemed a little unsteady on his seventy-two-year-old legs, and the expression on his eternally stoic face leaned more toward nervous.

"It does seem," he said, in a voice on the dry side of phlegmy, "a little melodramatic."

"Oh, I know," Gladys giggled, "but I was just so angry at that horrible little woman. I mean, who was she to tell me no? I've waited my whole life to meet you. Well, now that's not true. I never dreamed I would have the chance, so I guess I can't really say I've been waiting for it. Never mind. You're here and that's all that matters. And it *has* to mean something. Now, I hope you don't take this the wrong way, Jake. But facts are facts. You aren't the biggest star that ever was — and that's not your fault. And I'm sure there are places you could go where people wouldn't even recognize you. But you didn't go to those places. You came here. To Denniter. To me."

"You know," Shackles said, a little shakily, "I don't pick the locations."

Gladys smiled like a rewarded school-child.

"Exactly," she said. "And that just makes everything the more significant. It's fate."

"Well, I must admit, it does seem fortuitous, my dear."

"You called me that yesterday," Gladys beamed. "When you touched my shoulder."

"Ah, yes. I remember."

"You gave it a squeeze and I almost collapsed."

"So sweet."

"And then that woman." Gladys grew angry again. "Just because I've only got one winter coat."

"It's not right," Shackles tutted.

"People don't change their clothes every day. Well, I mean, of course they change their clothes, but they don't *change* their clothes."

"Of course." Shackles straightened himself and took a step forward. "Would you like me to do it again?"

"Sorry?"

"Your shoulder, sweet lady," the actor crooned, his voice like velvet sandpaper. "Shall I squeeze it once more?"

"Something has to be done. It's making him sick."

The smell of the dog's hot breath was enough to make Artie want to throw up. The woman had come sliding across the set with the animal wrapped in her arms. She shoved the lazy-lipped, milky-eyed beast right into his face. It smelled like old socks and there were long strings of saliva dangling from it snout.

"Maybe you could sweep some of it up," the woman continued. "Just a space big enough for Picasso to stand."

The dog sneezed, sending a spray of canine snot onto Artie's sleeve.

"Aw, for chrissakes, lady," he protested.

She went on as if nothing had happened. "It wouldn't have to be much more than a couple of feet wide."

Artie couldn't decide which to slap first, the lady or her mutt. So, instead, he plopped himself down in his chair. "Look," he said, dismissively, "I don't even know what the hell you're talking about." Then he turned to the shooting script: Christmas morning, Scrooge's enlightenment. The woman remained at his shoulder, her dog shuddering toward another sneeze.

"What is it, already?" he said, defeat seeping into his voice.

"It's Picasso," the woman said, in a tone reserved for foreigners and slow children. "He's eating the snow and it's making him sick."

Artie waited a moment. "And?"

"Well, I know how much you wanted him in the scene, so I thought if you just — "

"Wanted him in the scene?" Artie could feel his blood pressure rising. "Who the hell said I wanted him in the scene?"

The woman turned and pointed across the viscid set. "Why, he did."

Artie heard a snap in his head, somewhere just behind his ear. What it was he wasn't sure: patience, pride, that darkness that exists inside everyone but rarely emerges. All he was certain of was that when it popped, reason popped with it. He felt an instant heat, sweat began to leak from his entire body. He was out of his chair, out of his parka, and halfway across the set before he even realized he was moving. The veins in his neck and temples throbbed. Anger swelled in his knuckles. He didn't care anymore.

Adam Bickerstaff spun around on the soapy snow, his arms flailing for something to steady himself. He needn't have worried, Artie had a firm grip of him, pulling the shoulders of his ski jacket so tightly together the kid looked almost to be folded lengthwise. The blood had drained from his face, even from the mountainous peaks of his acne. Little snowflakes of Artie's spittle came to rest on the boy's blanched complexion.

"Who's the bloody director here?" Artie bellowed. "Eh?"

"Why, it's you, Artie," Bickerstaff squeaked.

"And who decides what goes in shot?"

"You."

"That's right."

He could strangle him, right there on the set, in front of everyone. Wrap his hands around that pimply neck and squeeze. Squeeze until the breath ran out of him. Who would care? The little low-life sycophant, who would really care if he choked the life out of his worthless waste of skin? Just the thought of it excited him. And then he stopped. The kid was crying, actually weeping.

"Where's Shackles?" Artie muttered.

"I knocked," the kid snivelled, "I knocked on his trailer, but," another snotty breath, "but there was no answer."

"Right," Artie said, another crack sounding in his skull. "you get rid of that woman and her dog or I'll fire your ass."

Then he turned and stalked off the set. People gave him a wide berth.

"Thinks he can screw on my time, does he," Artie growled.

It had not been an embrace, as Gladys expected; hadn't been the passionate pillow-kiss accompanied by the symphonic swell of pirated Dvorák. Rather, what followed Jake Shackles roguish offer was a feeble attempt to overpower her. He leapt awkwardly, like an ancient and off-balanced cat, for the pistol in Gladys' left hand. Missing it completely, he crashed with a groan onto the thick pile carpet. Gladys, misunderstanding, tried to help the whimpering actor to his feet. With the madwoman stalker leaning over him, Shackles took the opportunity to wrap his failing hands around her throat.

Gladys could feel her face flush. Her ears were burning, just like they did when someone talked about you, or at least that's what her mother had believed. And suddenly she was on her back, looking straight into Jake Shackles' face. It was red, too. There were little pellets of sweat on his brow and top lip. And his breath was coming in quick, desperate pants. Like Bert, she thought. That's when she realized what was happening. He was choking her. Jake Shackles was actually choking her.

She tried to speak, but her voice wouldn't come. Then she lifted her knee. It landed somewhere soft, his belly she guessed because he coughed out in pain. His hands loosened for a moment and Gladys took in a breath. But before she had time to exhale, he'd tightened his grip again. This time he was swearing. The words dripped from his lips. They were so foul she could taste them and their ugliness collected in foamy bubbles at the corners of his mouth. But then they started to fade. Shackles' mouth kept contorting, his spit kept flying, but his sound waned. As did Gladys' vision. It seemed to be dissolving; the edges crumbling into blackness.

Gladys swung her arm. She heard quite clearly the smack of metal on bone and the surprised yelp. Shackles rolled away immediately, clutching his withered hands to his head. It only took a few moments for Gladys' faculties to return. And when they did, she sat herself up and looked across at Shackles. He was cowering beside the Westinghouse propane powered cooker-range, a trickle of blood leaking from the scratch on his forehead.

"I'm bleeding," he wailed, all the leathery toughness

gone from his voice. "Oh my God, I'm bleeding."

Gladys got to her feet. Jake Shackles began to weep.

"You're nothing," she said, looking down at him.

"Oh, please," Shackles cried, his body all a palsy. "Oh, please. Don't kill me."

Neither of them heard the key in the door.

It was a pop, nothing more. Not even as loud as a fircracker. Peckinpah had been wrong. All the crashing and banging he'd used in *The Wild Bunch* and *Pat Garret and Billy the Kid*, it was too much. That innocent little pop was frightening enough. And the pain was frightening, too. Not like Artie had expected. It was a burning, like a hot poker. The worst thing, though, was being able to see it. The hole, about the size of a shirt-button, in his thigh.

With the key he wasn't supposed to have, Artie'd unlocked Jake Shackles' trailer door, stepped inside and seen the woman with the gun. He remembered thinking, *why do they have their clothes on?* Then the pop, the burning, the hole, the blood. Then he passed out.

When he regained consciousness, Artie Phritter was lying on the cold ground out front of the wardrobe truck. There were too many faces for him to register any. He felt extremely light-headed, like that time in Mexico, when he and Sam had smoked with the old man in the cantina. A voice he recognized said something about saving Jake Shackles. And then something about the press. Artie struggled to sit up, but a hand on his shoulder kept him down.

"The woman," Artie mumbled, his voice sounding far away.

"Don't you worry, Artie. The cops got her."

Adam Bickerstaff. He was kneeling beside Artie, holding his hand. A look of concern and opportunism on his face.

"My God, Artie. You're a hero."

And Artie Phritter smiled. A convict gaining his release. A sinner relieved of his penance. *Right*, he thought, *note to my agent.*

THE HONEYMOONERS

Harry stared out the window at the people passing by and wondered what they would look like dead. Would they be fatter, thinner, more handsome or less? Would their hair be neat? Would they look real? In eighty-seven years he'd never seen a dead body. Never been to a funeral or a wake where the casket was open; never witnessed a car accident; never saw anyone have a heart attack. When his father died, Harry was on a ship in the middle of the Atlantic, leaving England behind him forever. His sister found the old man in his bed, choked to death by his own lungs. When she died, the neighbours found her. Harry didn't return for either of the burials. There was no money then, even if there had been time. He didn't even get to see Samuel. Lizzy had found the child cold in the crib while Harry was at work. And by the time he made it home, the body was already gone. A week later he couldn't even remember what the boy had looked like. Just a baby, he told himself, not even in the house long enough to feel like a son. He never said so to Lizzy, though. She was devastated. She'd carried the child: nine months inside her; three days alive; and for fifty-seven years after his death. Now Lizzy was in the hospital. Four weeks already, maybe five. Harry couldn't be sure anymore. All he was certain of was that it was longer than they'd ever been apart.

He turned away from the window and checked his watch, then looked at the duffel bag on the sofa. All packed and ready to go: grey suit, black socks, white shirt, red tie, polished brogues, Lizzy's dress. He put his hand to his breast pocket and felt the brochure. Then he heard the toilet flush and Jack's heavy shoes cross the kitchen linoleum.

"Ready to go, Grandpa?"

Harry looked at his grandson standing in the living room doorway.

"How many times I have to tell you?" he said. "I'm goddamn deaf. You want to say something to me, you yell."

"I just asked," Jack said loud and slow, "are you ready to go?"

"I heard you, for chrissakes. And don't talk to me like I'm an idiot. Grab the bag and let's get out of here."

Harry started to the front door with a grimace on his face. He couldn't understand his grandson, nor any of his grandchildren for that matter. He'd always been uncomfortable around them and this stiffness aggravated him. Lizzy had never liked the way he spoke to them. She told him that they thought he was mean, simple as that.

"You're mean, Harry," she'd said over her knitting. "Mean and spiteful. And if you're not careful those kids will end up hating you."

"Let them hate me. Least then they'll be doing something. Instead of walking around like flunkies waiting for a kick up the backside."

"You say that now," she said with the smirk he missed so much. "But when I'm gone, you think they're going to come and visit you?"

"They'll be dancing on my grave long before they're weeping over yours, my sweet. Don't you worry about that. Besides, they only come to see us because their parents make them."

"Oh, Harry," Lizzy had said. "That's nonsense."

"Dearheart, they think we smell."

It was his granddaughter who'd said it, that she thought they smelled. Harry had been sitting in the living room watching the television with the sound turned off. She was in the kitchen with her mother and didn't know he was listening. She'd said they smelled old: like bread when it goes green. Harry had thought it was funny, until he heard the slap. He'd never hit any of his children. He looked over at Jack fumbling with the keys.

"It's the square one, sunshine. You're going to want to stick it in the ignition and turn."

Jack's face flushed.

"Why don't we take my car, Grandpa. I'd feel more comfortable if we did."

"That makes one of us."

"I'm not even insured to drive this," Jack muttered.

"You whine a lot, don't you, kid?"

Harry leaned his head back and closed his eyes and listened to the keys jingle between Jack's fingers. He prayed silently that the car would start. It hadn't been on the road in nearly a year and half. Not since he'd failed his last driver's test. Too slow, the examiner had said. Harry told him that he could drive faster, but the man had just smiled and shook his head.

The engine caught the first time. It was like a small weight being lifted from his shoulders. Harry kept his eyes closed as Jack eased the car out of the driveway. He let his fingers tap out a tally on his thigh as he went through the contents of the duffel bag in his mind. Everything was there. And why wouldn't it be? Lizzy had packed it carefully away in a trunk in the attic; all of it neatly folded, with tissue paper between each layer and mothballs scattered throughout. He didn't have to go searching for anything.

"Jesus Christ!" Harry bolted forward, the seatbelt digging into his shoulder. "Stop the car!"

"What is it? Your heart?"

"No, it's not my goddamn heart. Turn the car around. We have to go back."

"What did you forget?" Jack said. "Is it your pills?"

"Just go back, for chrissakes."

Harry made Jack wait in the car while he rifled through the bookshelf in the living room. He took down the Bible and let the pages run through his fingers. Then he did the same with the dictionary and the encyclopedias and the cookbooks, and the Royal Family pictorials. All were empty. Then, just as he was about to give up and go check in the bedroom, he found it. The dry brown stem was peaking out from between two books, the paperback romances that Lizzy loved so much. She must have taken it out to look at, then forgotten where it had come from; or, Harry thought, forgotten what it was.

Very carefully he pulled down the two novels, holding them together until he set them on the coffee table. He lifted the top one and put it aside, then picked up the boutonniere. It was as light as dust and he could see the thin vein-like cracks running through the parched umber petals of the rose. Harry took the brochure from his breast pocket and gently slipped the flower between its folds.

He said nothing to Jack when he got back into the car. Just made a motion with his hands and they started on their way. Harry watched the town as it slipped by the passenger window. The new aluminum-sided houses crammed in between the old stone homesteads; the post office where he walked everyday his legs would let him, to look into his empty post box; the library that used to be the Queen's Hotel. It took only a few minutes to pass through the place in which Harry had spent the last sixty-three years of his life and he wondered if Lizzy had noticed the same thing when the ambulance brought her this way. Not likely, he told himself. She was in too much pain. Harry could see her tears again as the paramedic slipped the oxygen mask over her mouth and he pushed the thought from his mind.

"So," Jack asked, "you going to tell me what that was all about?"

"Nope."

"Didn't think so."

Harry twisted himself on the seat to get a look at his grandson.

"You smoke?" he asked Jack.

"Smoke?" Jack said. "No. No, I don't smoke."

"Why the hell not?"

"Because cigarettes will kill you."

Harry laughed. "Jesus Christ," he said. "I smoked nearly my whole life and I'm eighty-eight goddam years old."

"Eighty-seven," Jack said.

"Huh?'

"You're only eighty-seven, Grandpa."

"What, are you keeping count or something? Shut up and drive."

Harry studied his grandson. Jack's hair was cut short, no sideburns, clean shaven; his shirt was pressed and tucked in, the creases in his trousers ran straight across the top of his knees, and his aftershave was blandly inoffensive. All of his grandchildren were like that. Nothing out of place, nothing daring. Why couldn't he have at least one who wore jackboots, or had forearms carved with tattoos; or one who had every fleshy appendage pierced? Like the kids he saw on TV; the ones on the news who tied themselves to trees and bulldozers. Why did they all have to be so boring? He was never like that. When he first met *Lizzy* he used to drink and fight *and* smoke. He wore his hat drooping over his eye, he swaggered. And she liked it, said he looked dashing. Hell, even his own kids got into their fare share of scrapes. The boys would come home boozy and bruised. The girls would roll their skirts above their knees as soon as they left the house. And what came of all that? Safety: monotonous, consistent.

"You drink, don't you?" Harry said.

Jack looked at him sideways, then nodded. "Yeah, sure," he said. "I drink a bit."

"Well, praise the Lord. You got any money on you?"

"A couple bucks. Why?"

"What's a couple."

"I don't know," Jack shrugged. "Twenty maybe."

"That's a lot of couple."

Jack tilted his head slightly, not wanting to take his eyes off the road. "You figuring on doing some shopping?"

"I thought we might stop for a drink," Harry said.

"Afraid not," Jack said. "I told mother we'd be at the hospital by three."

"Look here, bright eyes," Harry said, straightening up in the seat. "There's a hotel coming up in a few miles and it's got a bar in it."

"So?" Jack said.

"So, I'm going to have a drink there before I go to the hospital."

"Not possible."

"Listen, kid," Harry said, "you can come along if you like. Or you can keep going on your way and try explaining to your mother why I'm not with you. It's your choice, because when we get to that hotel, I'm getting out. And I don't care if this heap's going six miles an hour, or sixty."

Jack shook his head. "I get your point," he said. "Why don't we stop for a drink?"

"Now there's an idea."

Harry had the passenger door open and was swinging his feet toward the pavement before the car had even stopped. But when he stood up he could feel the twinge in his chest and thought about the glycerin tablets he'd left on the bedside table. He'd promised himself that he wasn't going to bring them, they didn't belong on the trip. But for the briefest moment he wondered if he'd been mistaken, foolish even. Then the pain passed and he knew he was right.

Jack waited for a tractor-trailer to pass by on the driver's side of the car, then stepped carefully out onto the road. He propped his elbows on the roof and peered across at Harry.

"Don't just stand there, sunshine," Harry said without looking at him. "Get the bag."

Harry didn't wait, but walked into the hotel. The lobby was just as he expected it to be, just like the old Queen's back in Orton. Jack almost bumped into him in the gloom. The man sitting behind the reception desk looked up from his newspaper and waited for one of them to speak.

"The bar?" Harry asked.

"End of the hall," the man said in a bored, flat voice and went back to his paper.

The hotel's lounge was as dark and empty as its lobby, but with the distinct odour of stale beer wafting from the carpeting. Harry crossed to the bar and settled himself down on a stool. Jack dropped the duffel bag on the floor and stood waiting.

"Sit down, for chrissakes," Harry said. "And give me your money."

"Remember," Jack said, "just one."

"I know, I heard you."

Reluctantly, Jack sat down and fished his money out of the front pocket of his trousers. The young woman behind the counter was flipping through a magazine, oblivious to their presence. "Excuse me, darling," Harry said.

She looked up, the same disinterested expression on her face as the clerk.

"What can I get you?" she said without moving.

"A new ticker would be nice."

The bartender gave Harry a stupid look.

"That was a joke," he said.

She shrugged her shoulders, "Whatever."

"Two beers will be fine," Jack said.

The beer tasted better than Harry could remember: cold and sharp, with just a faint tang of dishwashing detergent. It had been ages since he'd been in a real bar and it felt good to be back. He'd stopped going to the old Queen's when they shipped out the bottles and moved in the books. A goddamn library. It was like the temperance movement all over again. Of course, Lizzy wasn't all that upset about the change. She'd been complaining for years that the town needed a proper library. She was tired of the kids having to bring books down from the city. It was kind of them, yes. And she read whatever they brought. But it wasn't the same as going through the stacks yourself, she told Harry.

"Sometimes you just want to pick up something different," she'd said. "Something you're not expected to."

"You mean something dirty."

"Maybe I do, yes. Maybe I do."

Lizzy had read to him aloud from one of those dirty books. It had a black cover, with just the shadow of a naked body across it. They were in separate beds then, but it didn't matter, the words didn't spark any amorous feelings in them. They made them laugh, more than they had in a long time. And when Harry suggested that maybe they should give some of the positions a try, Lizzy said she didn't think he had enough pills left in his prescription to get him through. That made Harry laugh even harder.

"Hey, kid," Harry said, "you ever read any dirty books?"

Jack almost spit his beer out on the bar.

"What!?"

"You know. Magazines, novels. You ever read them or not?"

"What on earth are you talking about?"

"How about movies?" Harry went on. "You ever seen any of those blue movies? You know if I were your age — and I was once — I'd be grabbing everything I could get my hands on. We didn't have any of that stuff when I was a kid. I sure as hell wish we did. Would've saved a lot of embarrassment, I can tell you that. Least then I'd have known what everything looked like."

"Whoa, Grandpa," Jack said. "I think you've lost it."

"What the hell are you talking about, *lost it*?" Harry said. "I'm trying to have a conversation. You got a problem with that?"

"No. I don't. I just think maybe you should gear it more toward the matters at hand."

"Matters at hand? What's that supposed to mean? There are no matters at hand."

Jack stared at him.

"Forget it, kid," Harry said. "Drink your beer."

They were quiet for a few moments, then Harry turned back to Jack.

"I just thought it'd be nice to talk," he said. "I never get to talk to my grandkids."

Jack took a large mouthful from his glass, then he replaced it carefully onto the coaster. After he swallowed, he faced Harry.

"Maybe," he said slowly, "that's because you never liked any of your grandkids."

"Who the hell told you that?" Harry blurted.

"You, Grandpa," Jack said. "You told me. You told all of us. When we were just little."

Harry shook his head.

"You don't even remember, do you?" Jack said.

"If I said it, I didn't mean it."

"You might have known that, but we never did."

"Well, if any of you had a brain between you, you'd have known."

Jack laughed dryly. Harry looked down the bar to the young woman and raised his fingers.

"Two more," he said.

"I said we were only having one," Jack said.

"And I didn't listen to you," Harry said.

As Harry started on his second beer he thought about what Lizzy had always said to him; about how the kids would hate him when she was gone. He'd never believed her. Or if he did, he never believed there would ever be a time when he was here and she was not. The second beer didn't taste as good as the first.

"Fine," Harry said. "So I never liked you when you were a kid. Big deal. You ain't a kid anymore, right. Let's start fresh."

Jack sighed. "All right. Fine."

"Good," Harry said. "So, you got a girlfriend?"

"No."

"What are you, queer or something?"

"My God," Jack said. "You're unbelievable."

"What?" Harry protested. "What did I say?"

"Forget it."

"I'm just asking a question. You don't have a

girlfriend, so maybe you got a boyfriend. It happens, you know."

"Yes," Jack said. "I know it happens. But not to me."

"That's fine," Harry said. "I'm just saying that if you did like boys that would be fine too. Either way. You do what you like."

"I like girls."

"Okay."

Harry sipped at his beer. The slight twinge was returning to his chest. He shifted himself on the barstool and coughed a few times to cover his discomfort. He looked down at the duffel bag on the floor between him and Jack.

Then, quietly, as if his voice were coming from nowhere, he said, "Your grandmother was a very beautiful woman when I met her. Very beautiful."

Jack turned slowly to look at him, his bottle halfway to his lips.

"Are you okay, Grandpa?"

Harry eased himself off the stool and picked up the duffel bag.

"I got to go to the shitter," he said.

Harry missed the door to the men's room and ended up in the lobby again. This time the clerk didn't even bother to look up from his paper. Back in the gloomy passageway, Harry found the door and pushed through. Inside the smell of stale beer was replaced by that of fermenting urine. He stopped for a moment and sniffed deeply. The scent brought a warm glow of nostalgia and he thought of the old Queen's again. Then he searched for a dry section of floor and put down the duffel bag. Very carefully, he began to remove the clothes and hang them neatly on a stall door; then he started to undress.

When he reached his skivvies, Harry turned round and studied himself in the mirror. It wasn't something he normally liked doing. He found it disconcerting to see how much his body had decayed. The skin hung loosely off his once six-foot frame, the colour of rice paper. He could see the veins running purple-blue just below the surface. The dark wiry hair that used to cover his chest had grown ivory white and patchy. Even his breasts, which had always been flat against his body, drooped. Like those poor African mothers on the news, he thought, their milk all dried up. He was just happy he didn't have to change his underpants. The last thing he wanted to see today was his shrivelled, useless prick.

He took down his shirt first and slipped it on. The scent of mothballs floated from the fabric. He would have to leave the window open in the car to air it out. Next he took down the tie and began to slot a perfect Windsor knot. Manouevering the silk hurt his fingers, but he ignored the pain. Lizzy couldn't stand half-Windsors. Every time he had tried getting away with one, she would stand behind him and retie it for him. "The rabbit comes out of his hole," she would say. Harry mouthed the words. Then he pulled on the pants and the jacket. Everything hung as loosely as his own skin. Even his shoes were too big. I'm goddamn shrinking, he thought.

When he was finally dressed, Harry looked at himself in the mirror again. His heart sank slightly. He'd looked at the picture on the nighttable earlier that morning and imagined that once he had the clothes on, he would look as he had then. But he did not. There was a shadow of his former self in the mirror, but that was it. Just a shadow. He turned away from himself and picked up his cast off clothing. After he retrieved the brochure from his shirt pocket, he threw the lot into the garbage pail against the wall. Then he picked up the duffel bag with Lizzy's dress still inside.

Jack was waiting in the hallway outside the restroom, leaning against the far wall. Through the shadows Harry could see the stunned look on his face.

"Grandpa," Jack said, "where are your clothes?"

"In the bin where they belong."

"I don't understand."

"No," Harry said. "I don't suppose you do."

Back in the car, Harry was quiet. He watched the world fly by the window. He knew the way to the hospital like he knew the pattern of liver spots on the backs of Lizzy's hands. He'd been there enough with his bum heart. And as the car came over the crest of the hill that lead down to the parking lot, he felt his stomach begin to turn in anticipation. It felt like too much coffee swirling around in his belly in search of release and it pressed hard against his bladder. He half expected one of his daughters to be standing guard at the entrance waiting for them, ready to scold their tardiness. But there was no one there when they pulled up. He glanced up at the windows, but they were empty, as well

"Right, sunshine," Harry said, after they stepped from the car. "I want you to wait here."

Jack looked at Harry. He hadn't said anything to his grandfather since he'd come out of the washroom at the hotel. Now he let his eyes run over the strange clothes, then he reached out and brushed some fluff off the shoulder of the jacket.

"What are you doing, Grandpa?" he asked in a clear, serious voice. "Will you please tell me why you changed your clothes?"

Harry had to fight a sudden urge to hug Jack. A small wave of guilt washed over him. He'd known since they'd left the house, had known for weeks, what he was going to do, but he'd said nothing to his grandson.

He hadn't thought he could trust him. He still wasn't sure. But slowly he reached into his pocket and pulled out the brochure. He took the boutonniere from the folds and handed the pamphlet to Jack.

"Have a look," he said as he carefully slipped the dead flower into his button hole.

"What's this?" Jack said.

"That's where I'm taking your grandmother," Harry said.

"I beg your pardon?"

"I'm taking her there. It's where she always wanted to go. Where *we* always wanted to go. But we never got the chance. First there was no money. Then there were the kids. Then we forgot about it for a long time." Harry cleared his throat. "Now we're going."

"But Grandpa — "

"That's it. I don't want to talk about it anymore," Harry said. "You wait for me here, okay."

"Grandpa?"

"Wait here."

"I'll come up with you," Jack said quietly.

"Fine," Harry said and touched Jack's arm. "Fine. You come along."

Harry felt the cold as soon as he pushed through the doors. It was everywhere. It came up through the floor and out of the walls; it poured down in the bright white of the flourescent strip lighting; it lived in the air. The cold was what Harry hated most about hospitals, not the smell or the efficient cleanliness that bothered other people, but the cold. It was worse than deepest February. Whenever he'd been admitted for his heart, he always made sure that Lizzy brought him blankets from home, the thick wool ones that she knitted while they watched television; the ones she always gave to the grandchildren at Christmas. For a moment he regretted not having brought one for her, then he remembered that she wouldn't need it.

He stepped into the elevator and took the chill into his lungs. He didn't want Jack to see him shiver, so he shuffled his feet, then moved closer to his grandson, hoping to steal some of his warmth.

"What room is she in?" he asked.

"Four-ten," Jack said without looking at him.

"Not the number, that won't do me any good. Where is it?"

"You go left down the hallway and it's the last one on the right."

"Good," Harry said, "good." He bent down and opened the duffel bag. He could feel Jack watching him as he pulled out Lizzy's dress. The folds fell away as he straightened. The cream of the lace and silk had faded into a dusty yellow and a small tear had loosened the threads along part of the hem. But the beauty of it was still there. It held their day more clearly than the photograph on the night table.

"Grandpa," Jack said quietly, "do you know what you're doing?"

"Of course," Harry said. "What your grandmother and I have always wanted."

"But you haven't seen her since she's been here."

"What? I'm going to forget what she looks like?"

"She's changed, Grandpa."

"Jack," Harry said, folding the dress over his arm. "I've been married to Lizzy for over sixty years. I know her better than I do myself."

The elevator door opened to Jack's mother standing with her hands on her hips.

"Do you know how late you two are?" she demanded. She stopped when she saw Harry, the suit hanging like old drapes from his body. "Why in God's name are you dressed like that?"

Harry put out a hand to stop the elevator door from closing.

"Make a hole, darling," he said. "I'm coming through."

She didn't move.

"Let him by, Mom," Jack said.

Her son's voice heightened the look of disgust on her face and she leaned in toward Harry.

"My God," she said. "Is that beer I smell?"

"It most certainly is," Harry said.

"You've been drinking?"

"By the gallon," Harry said. "I can hardly stand up."

"You—"

"Leave it, mother," Jack said. "All right? Just leave it."

Harry turned and smiled at his grandson, then stepped out of the elevator. Jack was close behind him.

"This way?" Harry asked pointing down the hallway.

"Yes."

"Give me the brochure."

Jack held it out to him, but refused to release it when Harry tried to pull it away.

"Can I come with you?" Jack asked.

Harry stopped a moment and looked deep into his grandson's eyes. "Of course," he said. "Of course, you can."

Jack turned slowly to his mother and spoke with an authority that helped thaw Harry's chill. "I don't want anyone to disturb us," he said, then he took Harry by the arm and began to lead him down the hallway.

Jack's hand was comforting on the inside of Harry's elbow. It helped him to keep moving his feet as they grew heavier with each step. The boy was so much stronger than he looked, Harry thought. Then they stopped.

"We're here," Jack said.

Harry looked around him, then at the door. It was half closed, a little paper tag slid into the metal slot at eye level read: Elizabeth Burns. Through the crack he could see the foot of the bed.

"Would you like me to come in with you?" Jack asked.

Harry turned to Jack, realizing for the first time that his grandson was taller than he was. He nodded and tried to say yes, but the word wouldn't come.

Jack pushed the door open and let Harry step through.

Lizzy lay on her back with the covers pulled tight under her chin. Her face was turned toward the window.

"Lizzy," Harry whispered.

She made no movement.

"Lizzy, sweet. It's me."

Harry felt Jack's hand gently touch the small of his back.

"Look what I brought you," he said, and held the dress in front of him.

She turned her face slowly toward them.

"And look," Harry said quickly, "look at this." He held out the brochure and tried to laugh. "You said I'd forget, but I didn't. See, all your harping paid off." He turned and handed the dress to Jack, then moved closer to the bed.

"It's all set. I called the hotel last week. When I knew I was going to come for sure."

Lizzy stared at him with cold grey eyes.

"I've got it all worked out, dearheart. I'll just send Jack here for the chaplain, and while he's doing that I'll help you on with your dress. Just like before. Only this time I won't tickle you. I promise. I'll do it properly, okay?"

Harry could feel himself weakening.

"And then we can go," Harry said. "We'll say our 'I do's,' and then we're on our way. Jack can drive us. He'll be our chauffeur. You and I can sit in the back seat and sip champagne. We'll stop for a bottle on the way. We can sip champagne and not worry about a thing. And before you know it we'll be there. If you want we can go see the Falls first. Or we could go straight to the hotel and go and see them in the morning. Whatever you want. It's all set, dearheart."

Lizzy's mouth tightened and she turned her face back toward the window.

"Lizzy?" Harry said. "Did you hear me? I said, I'll send Jack now and then we can go. Lizzy?"

There was a long silence and Harry could feel the chill again. It moved up through his feet and began to shake in his knees.

"Lizzy, dear?"

"Go away," Lizzy said, her voice cracking like dead leaves. "Whoever you are, go away."

And everything was cold again. Cold and heavy. The weight of years collected in the loose creases of his wedding suit and pulled hard on Harry's bones. The brochure, at once paper thin, took on brick-like mass and slipped from his fingers. Even his blood seemed to slow. Then he heard Jack whisper to him and he felt his grandson's hand again, soft on his shoulder this time, pulling him gently back toward the door.

PINEAPPLES AND ALASKA

— for Charlotte, Georgina, Victoria and Maureen

"I do like a bit of pineapple," Jack said.

Sam looked down at the plate in his lap. The slices were cut thick and uneven. Black bits of rind clung to the pale yellow marrow where the dull knife had slipped. When Jack had asked if he'd wanted some, Sam hadn't realized he was being polite, hadn't realized that Jack was asking for himself. It caused unneeded embarrassment, heightened by the fact there was no pineapple in the house. The exchange of money was handled delicately on both parts: Sam offered to pay; Jack refused and pushed an extra five pounds into Sam's palm, in case he might like something else instead.

"How about you?"

"Yes," Sam nodded, "very much." He dug his fingernail under the slick edge of the thinnest piece and pried it like a wet coin from the plate. He'd gone straight to the kitchen when he got back from the greengrocer. He set the fruit on the counter and the change, including the extra fiver, on the table, then looked for a knife. Three drawers, quietly opened and searched, revealed nothing. So rather than continue to rummage, he took the cheese-stained bread knife from the sink and wiped the blade on a dishcloth. But standing over the tough-skinned fruit, Sam had no idea what to do. It was unfamiliar to him. Pineapple came from cans, already diced or in giant rings. No mess, no fuss. When he'd finished cutting, he knew the result was laughable. But Jack made no comment. He simply took the plate Sam held out to him and smiled a thank you.

"What are your plans for today?"

The acidy pulp leeched into Sam's tongue and the sourness locked his jaw. "London," he said, through clenched teeth.

Jack nodded and looked toward the television.

Sam set his plate down. "I've got to meet a few people tonight."

Jack nodded again and let the topic slip away. His fingers worked like thin, brittle twigs, sliding the moist flesh to the edge of the plate, until he was able to pinch it between thumb and index. From there it made the unsteady trip to his mouth. Juice ran over his bottom lip and dripped off his chin, but he made no move to wipe it away. He breathed heavily as he chewed.

Sam looked away from him to the television. Two bears, large and brown, stood in a fast flowing river at the lip of a small waterfall. From the froth below, the occasional salmon leapt. The bears swung half-heartedly at them. The sound was tuned low and the narration was muffled.

"Looks like your parts, that does," Jack said, motioning to the screen.

Sam shifted himself forward on the settee. "Somewhere out west," he said. "Rockies, maybe."

"They're big buggers, they are."

Sam agreed. They sat there, kitty-cornered in the lounge, and watched the bears ignore each other in the wilderness. Sam struggled to find something to say and wondered if Jack was doing the same. He pushed his hands together, allowed his fingers to mesh, then turned his wrists over and cracked his knuckles. The noise of his snapping joints seemed deafening. He spoke to fill the following silence.

"Bears scare the hell out of me," Sam ventured. "Not that I've ever seen one. Saw tracks once. Outside a friend's cabin. Well, it was her father's cabin, actually. I was just a kid. And they would've been black bears, anyway. Not near as big as these."

It was quiet again. There was only one bear now, running its claws through the bark of a tree. Jack slid the last of the pineapple into his mouth, then leant carefully forward and set his plate on the floor. He looked smaller after he straightened. His breathing was shallower, more laboured.

Everything felt awkward to Sam. He knew Jack was thinking, that he'd probably been thinking the whole time, even while they were talking. He also knew that whatever Jack's thoughts were, he played no part in them. He was there simply to keep him company: someone to speak to when Jack was ready to speak; a sounding board. The memories Jack played over and over again in his head did not include Sam, could not include him. He was a friend of Jack's daughter. A foreigner who stopped off for a few days whenever he found himself in England.

"They're more dangerous," Jack said.

"Sorry?"

"Black bears," Jack continued. "They're the ones you have to watch out for. These here," he pointed at the television, "big browns, aren't such a problem. They've no natural enemies. Nothing to challenge them. Black bears are different. Smaller. Still, if you show a bear, any bear, the respect it deserves—"

"Oh, I respect them," Sam smiled.

"Fear is not the same as respect."

The words fell almost cold from Jack's lips. And Sam felt as if they were directed not so much at himself as the purpose he was serving: words formed by Jack's tongue for the benefit of Jack's ears.

"You've got to understand something to respect it," Jack continued. "You can still fear something you understand, but it's a different kind of fear. Rational. Just being afraid makes the danger greater."

Jack was looking past the television now through the French windows that gave onto the back garden. His stare was so consuming that for a moment Sam considered getting up and opening the doors, thinking that Jack might want to feel the light breeze that was rustling the leaves of the tall oak beyond the stone patio. But when he turned back Jack was no longer looking through the windows. His head was tilted to the side and he was studying the loose folds of skin that sagged from his forearm.

"Did you know," Jack said, as if to his own flesh, "that in Alaska they say the blossoms of the forget-me-not are the colour of Frank Sinatra's eyes? And the fireweed can grow to seven feet high, covered in pink flowers from top to bottom. Then there's the larkspur and the saxifrage and the primrose and the yarrow. There's more colour there than in the finest English garden. Did you know that?"

"I didn't," Sam shook his head. "It sounds wonderful, though."

"Oh, it is."

"I didn't know that you'd been," Sam said, leaning forward again.

"I haven't," Jack said.

"Well, you never know." Sam immediately wished he could retrieve his words. Jack let them pass with a soft smile, and looked again toward the garden.

"Your Red Indians," Jack said, "I'm not sure which

ones, have a legend about how their people came to be in America. They say that their ancestors in Siberia helped one giant to slay another and the dead giant's body fell across the Bering Sea. They walked across his corpse into the New World. But over time his body decomposed until it was covered over again by the water. Except for the Aleutian Islands. That's the only part of his skeleton still visible." Jack let out a long sigh. "Russian fur traders killed most of the Aleutians."

Sam nodded, not sure how to respond. He wanted to say that a lot of that type of thing had gone on then,and that it was truly awful. Instead, he picked up his plate again.

"Would you like the rest of my pineapple?" he asked.

"Only if you don't want it."

"I've had my fill, I think," Sam said. "I could cut more."

"No. That's fine," Jack said, taking the plate. "My stomach couldn't take much more than this."

A silence drifted over them once again while Jack's wasted fingers worked to grip the slick fruit. On the television, the lone bear was preparing its den as the first flakes of winter snow twisted their way through the darkening sky.

"They don't hibernate," Jack said, after he swallowed the last of the pineapple. "At least not what we would think of as hibernation. Sure they sleep like the dead for weeks on end, but never for an entire winter. I'll wager you didn't know that either?"

"I didn't," Sam said.

"It's true," Jack nodded. "They get hungry or restless. And the sows give birth in winter. But sometimes they just get lonely. I like that, that they sometimes just get lonely." Jack smiled. "See what I mean about understanding them?"

Sam looked at Jack's smile and understood its loneliness: wan, penultimate.

"So, Jack," he said, "why Alaska?"

"Moira asks me that all the time."

The touch of his wife's name on his lips changed the nature of Jack's smile, imbued it with memory and companionship, filled it with life.

"Why Alaska?" he said softly. "The contradictions, I expect. The fact that to most people it's a wasteland. A never-ending tract of barrens. A desert of snow and ice. But it is so much more. There are trees there as big as California redwoods. Coastal rainforests that rival the Amazon. Mount McKinley climbs twenty thousand feet into the sky and the Aluetian Trench plunges twenty-five thousand below the sea. There's wildlife that has ceased to exist anywhere else. It's almost as if time has stopped there. In some places the sun doesn't set for three months. Just hangs in the sky, as if it were on a string, barely moving. Stretching a single day to half a year. Imagine that. Our time, clock time, watch time, becomes nothing more than numbers. But real *time...* well, real time..."

The redness in Jack's face brought small tears of sweat to his brow. His voice rattled into silence and his body sagged inward.

"Glacial ice covers only three percent of the entire state," he said, the words barely whispered. "Three percent. If Alaska were a person, the ice would take up no more space than the liver."

He paused.

"I think I'd like some tea, Sam," he said. "Do you think you could make me some tea?"

"Of course."

In the kitchen Sam filled the kettle, then searched through the cupboards for cups and saucers. The teabags were in a ceramic container at the back of the counter. As he reached for them, he noticed the pineapple, its juice leaking out and pooling on the scored cutting board. He found cellophane beside the bread box and wrapped it tightly around the fruit, then slipped it into the refrigerator. Looking through the small galley-window that gave onto the lounge, he saw that Jack had settled back on the settee. His eyes were closed. Sam sat down at the kitchen table, lit a cigarette, and listened to the water warming on the stove.

The phone, when it rang, startled him. Its tone like a hand shaking him out of his stupor. On the third ring he found the receiver, a small plastic frog nestled between the sugar bowl and butter dish. When he picked it up, the legs unfolded to reveal the mouthpiece.

"Hello?"

"Sam?" It was Jack's daughter. "What are you still doing there?"

"Making tea."

"What about your train?"

"I'll catch the next one."

"You didn't have to stay, you know."

"It's no problem," Sam said, lifting the kettle from the element. "We've been watching television."

There was a long silence.

"How's he been?"

"Okay, I think. Tired, but okay." Sam peeked through the galley-window again. "It looks like he's sleeping now."

"Let him be, then," she said. "My mom'll be home soon."

"All right."

"I've got to get back to work, but call us when you get down to London."

"I will."

Sam re-folded the legs of the frog and set it back in place. Then he put out his cigarette. The teapot, an oversized Brown Betty, sat on a tray on the sideboard.

Sam dropped three bags into it, filled it with hot water and replaced it on the tray along with the cups and saucers.

Jack was snoring lightly when Sam set the tray onto the coffee table. A small drop of foamy spittle collected in the slack corner of his mouth. On the wall above him was a small, silver-framed, black and white photograph. It showed Jack and Moira, years before. She wore a tight floral dress, her legs crossed at the ankles and feet pulled back under the chair. Jack had on a dark suit with a narrow tie, his chest ballooned with pride. Sam looked from the photograph to Jack, the muscles that had stretched that dark material now atrophied.

He poured himself a weak cup of tea and moved back to the other settee, sitting down carefully so as not to spill any. Jack shifted slightly on the cushions opposite him and let a soft moan slip through his lips, but did not awaken. Sam turned his attention again to the television. It looked to be early summer. Stark white credits slid quickly over a sow and her two cubs as they tumbled through long grass strewn with flowers: orange, blue and yellow. How far north was it? Sam wondered, as he passed his tongue across his bottom lip, tasting the last sugary sweetness of the pineapple.

COULD BE RAININ'

On the edge of the marshy stretch of bay, we floated silently, our worms bloated in the water, fruitlessly trying to tempt bass from the weeds. We had been without luck and this worried me; my father lived by a rule of no defeat. We would not leave until one of us had a strike.

The light was growing dim and the wind was building outside the sheltered bay. The tops of the trees that lined the shore shifted restlessly, and I could hear the murmur of waves chopping the water my father and I had to cross to return to the cottage.

I looked at my father through the greying air. His eyes were fixed on the tip of his fishing pole, waiting patiently for it to dip. I so badly wanted to shift myself; my rump had fallen asleep and was numb on the wooden bench in the bow. My hands were stiff. I flexed only my fingers and prayed silently that as the light died, so too would my father's resolve. At some point, even he would have to admit defeat and haul in his useless bait. With the clicking of his reel, I gained my freedom. Finally, I could stretch my aching limbs without fear of being exposed.

I leaned my head back and watched a crane glide silent overhead and come to rest precariously on a wavering limb at the shore's edge. Convinced it would find no rest on the swaying branches, it took once more to the air, passing above me again as it made its way across the bay. I watched as it dipped below the far tree-line and merged with the shadowy leaves of dusk. High above, a few remaining gulls were tossed about in the increasing currents of air. Around our boat the bay had begun to melt into itself.

"Enough's enough." My father's voice startled me. "Bring your line in, we'd best get goin'."

The worm I had struggled earlier to skewer with my hook was pale and swollen and crumbled like wet bread between my fingers. My father yanked hard on the pull-cord while I dispensed the few remaining strips of nightcrawler over the side of the boat. The tired Evinrude motor sputtered and died. He pulled hard again, opened the throttle wide and waited as the small motor sputtered again, then caught. He patiently revved the choking engine as I secured my hook in an eye halfway down my fishing rod. I carefully stowed my pole and took my place on the middle bench, and with my cap turned round backward, I faced front.

"All set?" my father asked.

I nodded and he took the engine out of neutral and started us toward the narrows. The motor whined quickly through the scale and pushed us swiftly across the placid bay. Travelling in such close proximity to water distorts the senses; we seemed to move unnaturally fast. The thick foliage surrounding us on both shores threw the noise of the small outboard back to our ears, making it sound larger than it was.

The temperature dropped noticeably as we neared the mouth of the bay. The wind carried a chill that forced me to double over, in search of warmth. I fixed my eyes on the loose rivets in the bottom of the boat. My father had caulked them repeatedly with clear silicone, but I could see the rippling pulse of the water seeping through with each small wave we slipped over. A small plastic pail, used to bail water, shuddered continuously between my feet.

I felt the boat slow. The high whine of the motor descended into a gurgling purr. Through the evening dim I could see the grey-white break of the waves as they crashed over the shoal running between the points which came together to protect the bay. The air, cold with spray, wet my face. We moved at a crawl.

"Get up front," my father said. "Keep an eye out for rocks."

I scrambled to the front bench, kneeled and leaned out over the bow. The water was loud and angry.

"Put your feet under the seat," my father yelled.

I listened to him and anchored my feet under the bench, then tipped myself over the bow again. The sun had all but vanished from the sky, leaving only meagre straggling rays to aid me. I strained my eyes and looked for the dark forms that I knew were just below the surface. The rocks were there, we'd picked our way through them innumerable times, but the water was thick and inky. Its depths impenetrable.

"I can't see anything," I called back to my father.

"Keep lookin'."

The waves were beginning to lift the prow; they broke large in the shallows. The bow would rise high on the crest, then slam down in the wake, digging into the following wave. The spray was thick and cold. I stared, searching for the shoal. But for the brief grey foam which burst in caps off the waves, I could see nothing. From the stern I could hear the motor choke deep in the water, then shriek as the prop broke surface.

"Anythin'?" my father called. The wind pushed his voice away from me.

"No."

I stole a quick glance toward the point on my left. We had barely entered the narrows. We were just coming onto the bay edge of the shoal. Still nothing, like a moonless night. The spray began to burn my face with its chill. Each time the bow slammed into the water the boat would cut deeper into the ensuing wave.

My father yelled something. It was swallowed by the roar of the lake. I turned to hear him better.

"Don't look at me, for chrissakes. Watch for rocks!"

His voice frightened me. Not because it was angry, but rather worried. I looked back into the churning waters, desperately wanting to see the shoal but at the same time afraid to find it. The rocks should've been there. They were there. We were on top of the shoal, I just couldn't see it. I lifted my head again, this time looking out into the lake before us. The sky was growing indigo, cloudless.

The next wave was quick and large. It rocked through the hull and lifted the boat high. The bow came down hard and deep and water broke clean over the prow, wetting my front. The engine gurgled and whined. We were halfway through the narrows, over the shallowest of the shoal. We foundered momentarily in the calm wake, then another wave hit, harder than the last. It struck at an awkward angle and wrenched the boat to port. I was pushed hard to the side, slamming my hip into the cold metal. More water rushed over the prow. My feet were soaked. I heard the engine gurgle once more, this time the whine did not follow.

"Shit!" My father's voice was strangely clear.

He whipped around on his seat and jerked furiously at the pull-cord. Nothing. Only the whir of the fly-wheel spinning loosely in the housing. The waves had turned the boat sideways and rolled it mercilessly over unsteady peaks and through shifting valleys. The spume of capping waves spilled over our sides. My father pulled once more, then stopped.

"Grab an oar."

His voice seemed to tear at his throat like the wind at the water.

I fought to free the oar lodged beneath my fishing pole. I pulled it loose and tried to fit its pin in the lock.

"Forget about that, godammit," my father hollered. "Just push off the bottom."

He was half-standing, half-kneeling on the stern bench, thrusting the oar straight down into the water, pushing off the shoal. In the plunging valleys between the waves his oar was never more than half submerged. Assuming my father's stance I pushed the oar, with all my strength, into the raging water. I fought the buoyancy of the wood and the temper of the breakers. For a brief moment, I felt bottom, only to have the oar thrown surface-ward again.

Steadily we were being pushed toward the craggy shoreline. I stabbed my oar once more into the churning surf, determined to touch the shoal. The wave bore down on us and tore the oar from my hands. I froze as it rolled away.

"Don't worry about it," my father called over his shoulder. "Get in the middle."

For a moment I couldn't move. Another wave slammed and again I was thrown painfully against the side of the boat. I slipped quickly to the middle bench and pulled myself tight. I watched my father steady himself, readjusting the plant of his foot. Over and over he dug his oar into the lather. He fought the current hard until he had the boat turned and facing into the bay. We lurched like driftwood back through the narrows. When he could no longer reach bottom, he began to paddle us toward the calmer waters.

Out of the narrows the touch of the wind seemed to

all but disappear. It no longer stung my face, but filled my ears. I could hear the waves hiss as they broke over the shoal. The further we moved into the bay the more distant their sound became, until it seemed no louder than the reverberations in a hollow conch. We drifted.

My father sat down, the oar resting across the gunnels. He looked down at his feet. For a long while we floated in silence. When he finally spoke, his voice was low, measured.

"I think we're gonna have to wait it out."

My first thought was how would we get back; we had entered night and our boat was without running lights. I wanted him to tell me.

"You all right?" he asked.

"Yes."

"Better drop anchor."

I moved to the bow and felt under the bench; it was getting too dark to see. I found the anchor and slipped it over the side. It found bottom quickly. I took hold of the side and led myself back to the middle.

"It's quiet," my father said after a moment.

"Yes."

The distant hush of the waves was joined by the soft purr of the anchor line as it gently crept over the edge.

My father lit a cigarette. In the glow of his lighter I saw his eyes shine tired and nervous. Then only the glow of his ash. He drew deeply.

"You cold?" he asked, exhaling.

"A little. Not bad." I was shivering.

"Want my jacket?"

"I'm fine." I was wet through my shirt, jeans and shoes.

I felt the boat shift gently as he made himself comfortable on the back bench.

"You get too cold..." His voice trailed off.

We were silent for a long while. Around us, all was

black. I pulled my arms from inside my sleeves and held them close to my stomach, warming them against my skin. I clenched my teeth to halt their chattering and wondered how long we would have to wait out here, floating. It wasn't safe to go anywhere through the dark without running lights, but even if we'd had them, I could still hear the faint grumbling of the angry water.

There was a splash off to the side. I shifted and peered into the night, hoping to discover what it was, or at least where. I heard my father's cigarette fizzle out in the water.

"Nice night, at least," my father whispered. It was not an attempt at humour. "Could be rainin'," he said, his tone unchanged.

I could feel the blueness in my lips and was worried that my shivering would echo through the boat; I didn't want my father to know how cold I was.

"My old man used to bring me fishin' out here when I was your age." He coughed to clear his throat.

"Really?"

I think he nodded.

"Too bad you never met him."

My grandfather's car had left the road and hit a tree before my parents were married. My father rarely spoke of him.

"He built the cottage we're stayin' in." His voice carried clearly over the few feet between us. He lit another cigarette and looked out over the darkened waters, toward the indistinguishable forest on the far shore.

"He drew up all the plans and his two older brothers helped him build it. Practically the first cottage on the big bay. The Jacksons' and the Stodders' were the only others."

My father's voice was comforting. I loosened my teeth and straightened slightly. I watched as the ember of his cigarette burned bright then softened as he smoked.

"He used to row us out here to fish. Like we are now. There wasn't any motors on the lake then. He never much liked them anyway. This bay was full of bass then, too. Not like now. A lot of it was still marsh. And because we didn't have a motor, we could sneak right into the reeds where the ones were."

My father stopped talking. My eyes had adjusted somewhat and I could make out his dark figure at the back of the boat, staring out over the water. I pulled my feet up onto the bench and wriggled my toes to keep them warm. He was quiet. There was another splash off to the side.

"It was just over on that shore somewhere," my father said, the burning tip of his cigarette waving over the black water. "Just along that shoreline where the Jackson kid... well, he ain't a kid no more. You know him, the old guy in the cottage near the point. Anyway, it was over there he hooked the sturgeon. I was probably about two, so I didn't see it, but my old man told me about it later. There was three of them out fishin'. My old man, the kid and Mr. Jackson. So, the old guy — the kid I mean, I think his name was Bobby. Well, we'll call him Bobby so it don't confuse things. So, Bobby hooks onto somethin'. And whatever it is, it don't budge. Like a snag. That's what they all figured it was, anyway. So, Mr. Jackson — the kid's father — tells him to cut his line. But Bobby ain't havin' none of that. It's his favourite lure, you see. But Mr. Jackson gets ready to cut the line anyway and this starts Bobby bawlin'. Then my old man turns to Mr. Jackson and says, Jim — I think that was his name — he says, Jim, if the kid likes the lure so goddamn much, drop him on shore so we can get on with our fishin'. Mr. Jackson's all for that. Bobby, too, of course. And they row in and drop the kid off. No sooner does Bobby get his feet on dry land and the snag starts to run. It's strippin' line off the reel like there's no tomorrow. Just whippin' it off. Off course, Mr. Jackson tries to take the rod, but do you think Bobby's gonna give that thing up? Not a snowball's chance in hell. He's set on bringin' it in, whatever it is. So the thing runs, the kid takes in some line, and the thing runs again. This goes on for hours. Run and reel, reel and run. I'm tellin' you, it's like somethin' outta one of them deep sea fishin' shows. Mr. Jackson say somethin' about cuttin' the line again and my old man turns to him and says, go right ahead, Jim, if you don't mind swimmin' your way home. A whole 'nother hour goes by before Bobby's got most of his line back. But the kid's dead tired and blattin' like a baby again. He's only got about fifteen, twenty feet of line left out but still they can't see what the hell's on the other end. And Bobby's ready to give up. Says his arms are killin' him, his back's sore, his hands are hurtin'. He can't take no more. So you know what my old man up and does? He says, you cut that line kid and I'll make sure you swim back with your pa. The funny thing is, it ain't even my old man's boat. It's the Jacksons'. But it don't make no difference. He could've threatened to cut the kid's legs off, because Bobby's still blubberin' away, sayin' he can't hold on anymore. Then, my old man turns to him and says, kid, you hold onto that rod for another two minutes and I guarantee whatever's on the other end'll be sittin' here at your feet. And he goes into the water. Walks right out, shoes, pants, everythin'. Just walks out. Don't even check and see how deep it is. He's got Bobby's line in one hand and the other out at his side for balance. He keeps his hand on the line even after it dips under water. When he gets about waist deep, he stops. Next thing you know he goddamn dives under. He's down there for, I don't know, pretty near three minutes. Then... BOOM! He comes up spittin' and gaspin', water flyin' everywhere, and he's got his arms wrapped around this monster sturgeon. Got to be four and a half, five feet long. Maybe sixty-five pounds. And he carries this thing in a big bear hug all the way back to shore, and drops it at the kid's feet. The thing was so goddamn big it took 'em ten minutes to kill the bugger. Had to keep bashin' it over the head with a big stone. It's even too big to put in the boat, for chrissakes. Wouldn't fit in there with the three of 'em. They had to tie it up with the anchor line and tow it back."

Then he stopped. There was silence again, complete now. Even the night noises had ceased. I looked off toward the shore where he stared, trying to imagine myself and the behemoth. I couldn't. The beast was too powerful. But I could see my father — could see him wading into the swampy water, disappearing beneath its surface.

When he spoke again, I closed my eyes to listen.

"We used to hunt ducks here, too." He spoke very slowly. "I'll bring you some day. Show you where my old man built his blind. He used to put it in the same spot every year. Down that little stream there at the end of the bay."

In my mind I could see where he pointed.

"The ducks would follow that stream down out of the marshes in the mornin'. Then follow it back up at dusk."

I'd never been hunting, but I could see myself in the boat. It was wedged into the tall reeds and covered over with dead bullrushes, waiting in the crisp morning twilight, the new sun burning the early mist, the squawk of the duck-call piercing the waking air, the strong smell of coffee-filled thermos flasks, and above, the faint shadows of mallards and teals in whistling flocks against the paling sky.

My father's voice droned in my ears and weighed heavy on my eyes.

"Wake up, son."

I shifted. My body was stiff, my eyes thick.

"Come on, son. Wake up."

It was bright. A blue-white ocean of sky above me. I could see my breath and hear the grumbling of the motor. While I had slept, he'd removed the cowling and dried the plugs with his shirt.

I sat up on the bench. My father's jacket was wrapped tightly around my shoulders. I looked at him. His smile was something I was not accustomed to seeing. He sat on the back bench with a cigarette dangling from his lips.

"Take this."

He passed me the oar.

"See if you can get the other one."

We were close to the rocks that ran along the shore of the right point. The motor idled and we drifted gently in. The water was so calm. I reached out with the one oar, heavy in my hands and pulled the other from the rocks, then leaned over the side and grabbed hold of it. The water was warm. My father took the oar from me and used it to push us back in the narrows.

"Best get yourself up front and look for rocks."

I moved slowly forward and felt the blood loosen my limbs. Perched over the bow I could see straight through to the bottom. The path was clear and I guided my father through the shoal and into the lake.

THE LONG WEEKEND

Sean Farrell could see the fireworks again, going off in his mind as his body sank further into the swamp. Roman candles exploded in yellow, orange and red corollas high above the lake, repeating themselves on the glass pane of its surface. The screams of the Catherine wheels seemed to fill his ears, making him deaf to the night creatures that surrounded him. He could feel the concussions in his chest, where they mixed with the whisky. But the stench that filled his nostrils was noxious.

The water wouldn't be deep. No higher than our shins, if that, he'd said to Shelley. Tie your laces tight so you don't lose your shoes in the mud. He'd told her that, too. Now the water was passing over his knees. It brought the mud up with it, like greedy hands from below, clutching at his legs.

Sean slid down in the kid leather seat and listened to the engine of the Saab purr down the highway. Marty's car always left him feeling ambivalent. Its smooth silver lines and Scandinavian weight caught his eye; he could see himself behind the tooled steering wheel, holding it white-knuckle tight as he took a corner at seventy-plus; sometimes he even longed for the pride and arrogance it would bring while he idled at the traffic lights and looked at the other cars idling beside him; the shitty cars. His car. But as Marty punched the accelerator, Sean knew that these were also the things he despised. And as he felt his body grow heavy in the seat, he hated the Saab again.

"I'm telling you, Sean," Marty said smiling at the power under his foot. "You gotta get yourself one of these babies. Just listen to it."

"Yeah, right."

"Of course, you'd have to find yourself a real job first." Marty laughed and punched the soft leather steering wheel. "No, seriously. I know a guy who can get you an eighty-two for four grand. It's a fucking steal. The thing's mint."

"Where the hell am I supposed get that kind of money?"

"I guess you'll have to save up your tips," Marty said and laughed again.

"Or maybe you could have a word with Daddy Warbucks?"

Marty turned to him and peered over his sunglasses.

Sean smiled and gazed out the window. He was desperate for a cigarette. He didn't have to look at the ashtray to know it was full of loose change, or that the lighter served as a hook for the air freshener that polluted the car. Marty forbade smoking. He'd made that clear the first time he took Sean for a ride. You can't get the stink out of the upholstery, he'd told him. So Sean had to make do with smelling the nicotine stains on his fingers.

Charbot Lake was a two and a half hour drive from Peterborough, but Marty was determined to cut an hour off the trip. As soon as they'd cleared the city he reached under the dashboard and switched on the radar detector. And except for the one beeping patch they'd just passed through, they never dropped below ninety. Sean rested his head against the window and watched the asphalt fly past. With anyone else he would have been nervous, but Marty was good with speed. He lived in a world of velocity. That was what had attracted Sean to him during their first year at university. Whereas he moved with a protraction that verged on sloth, Marty sprinted through everything. His feet were as fleet on the track as his mouth was in tutorials; and in both, he left Sean standing in the starting blocks. They were like the tortoise and the hare. But in their race, the hare always won.

It had been that way with Shelley, too. They saw her at the same time, across the lecture theatre. She'd looked over and smiled, but from such a distance it was impossible to tell at who. A few months later, when they were all quite drunk at Sean's apartment, Shelley admitted she'd grinned at both of them. He had no one but himself to blame that she'd ended up with Marty. While he'd been content just to watch her, Marty required action.

Marty fiddled with his wedding band as he steered the car gently along the potted dirt road. It wound for miles through the thick forest that cut the cottage off from the highway.

"I swear to God, Sean," Marty said. "I'm gonna pave this goddam thing. I don't give a shit what Shelley says. If it's the choice between saving a few fucking trees or this baby's suspension, then *tim-ber.*"

Everyone knew early on that Marty and Shelley would marry. Just waiting for the contract to be ratified, Marty used to say. The terms had been set by Shelley's father. They were simple: Marty was to finish his degree, then start work with her family's real estate business.

It was Sean who saw the engagement ring first. And when Marty showed it to him, the rock sparkled more paycheques than he could count. He saw it again the next night when Marty was out of town. Shelley had come round to his apartment and the two of them sat up drinking cheap red wine. She played with the ring most of the night, twisting the diamond to the inside of her finger and hiding it in her closed fist.

Sean fought with himself the whole evening to suppress the urges the wine introduced. And when Shelley, halfway into the third bottle, wondered how things might have been different had he, rather than Marty, shown up at her dorm, Sean did his best to force a smile.

They could see the smoke from the barbecue rising above the knoll that hid the cottage. Once over its crest they saw Shelley swatting at the flames with a spatula. The flagstone patio, which Sean had helped Marty build the previous summer, was awash with bodies. A mishmash of cars were parked in the clearing behind the cottage and Marty pulled the Saab in alongside them.

"Fuck me, do I hate these people," Marty said as he popped the trunk and began to load beer into Sean's waiting arms.

"If you hate it so much then why do it?"

"Tradition, man. Tradition. You can't let the July First weekend go by without the ol' Marty-Shelley shindig. Wouldn't be right."

"If you don't want them here, don't invite them."

"Wouldn't make any difference," Marty shrugged. "They'd come anyway." He loaded the last case of beer onto Sean, then opened the passenger door and rummaged round the back seat. When he re-emerged, he wore a broad smile and brandished a bottle of Glenfiddich. His eyes sparkled as he held it up.

"We'll let the morons drink the monkey piss," he said pointing at the beer. "You and I'll do it in style."

Sean loathed the annual gathering. The thought of sharing the company of people he'd often tried to avoid at school, having to listen to them add another layer of fiction to their trite student exploits, being regaled with stories of uptight bosses, cramped windowless offices, irritating neighbours, irresponsible babysitters, the price of children's Reeboks, was almost more than he could bear. Then there would be the pitying looks, the drunken slaps on the back, the derisive laughter when he explained, yet again, that yes, he was still waiting tables at the café; yes, he was still in the apartment on Hunter Street; yes, he was still single, free, unattached, alone. The only reason he bothered to come anymore was Shelley.

After they'd unloaded the Saab, they went into the back bedroom to change. Sean stood by while Marty picked out the proper attire for the both of them. They hadn't had time, according to Marty, to stop by his apartment and grab the duffel bag Sean had packed and waiting by the door. It had been straight out of the café and into the car. So he ended up standing to the side while Marty sifted through the bottom drawer of the bureau, pulling out cotton Jamz and Lacoste shirts until he was satisfied with their respective combinations.

"Here," Marty said pitching the clothes across the bed to Sean. "Now get out of that shirt. It fucking reeks."

Sean tried to keep his eyes averted as they dressed. He didn't want to see how well Marty had kept his body since their student days. He knew he would have to put up with it for the rest of the weekend: watching him flex like Mr. Universe at the edge of the dock before he leapt like a perfect swan; laughing with the others after

Marty scooped him up and tossed him in the lake; trying to suck in his enamel-white belly while Marty's glowed like a bronzed tympani.

"Jesus Christ, Sean. When's the last time you saw the sun?"

"I've been working a lot."

"Not on your abs, that's for sure."

Sean patted his tummy. "It's paid for."

"Well," Marty grinned, "looks like you bought a lemon. And a fucking pale one at that."

Sean took a warm Molson's onto the patio with him and leaned against the cottage wall, while Marty smiled and offered a glad hand to his guests. Shelley stood at the barbecue and sipped her Bacardi and Coke. Sean wanted to sneak up and wrap his arms around her, but she was deep in conversation. Besides, she already knew he was there. So instead, he sipped his tepid beer and started to peel the label from the bottle.

He felt strange in Marty's clothes, as if he were wearing an extra skin that didn't belong to him. When he'd caught sight of himself in the bedroom mirror, he was reminded of an altered photograph: his head pasted onto Marty's body. He couldn't deny that he looked better than usual, more stylish. But that's what made him feel awkward: others would notice, too. He plunged his hand into the front pocket of the shorts, hoping to find his cigarettes. He'd left them in his jeans.

"Jesus, Mary and Joseph."

Sean heard the voice float across the flagstones just as he was about to turn back into the cottage.

"Sean Farrell."

Pat Michaud pushed his premature jowls in Sean's direction.

"Goddammit. I haven't seen you in—"

"A year," Sean said.

"That's right," Pat said clamping a hand on Sean's

shoulder. "Christ, you don't look ... I don't know, more than—"

"A year older?"

"Ha! Perfect. You played right into the line, just like you read my mind."

"It's an open book, Pat."

"What's that?"

"Your mind."

"Ha! I love it! Perfect." Pat cracked his glass of vodka into Sean's bottle, almost shattering both. "Whoa," he said steadying himself. "I'm pissed."

"Only way to be," Sean said.

"You can say that again, my friend. You can say that again."

Sean did and Pat laughed again, then wrapped his arm around Sean and blew fermented Russian potatoes into his nose. "So, tell me. You're not still..."

Sean endured until Marty rescued him with a tug of the sleeve. He pulled him away from Pat and lead him back into the cottage. Ostensibly, they had retreated indoors to go over the logistics of the evening's fireworks display. Marty always did his best to outdo the previous summer. His goal was to produce a pyrotechnic extravaganza that would show those assembled how far he'd come since their days of essay writing and all-night cramming sessions; a *feu d'artifice* to draw the line between where he stood and where they longed to stand. But instead of digging out his crate of ordnance, Marty retrieved the whisky from the bedroom. He pulled two crystal tumblers down from the top shelf of the glass-fronted kitchen cupboard and loaded them with ice. Then poured two fingers of Glenfiddich in each and added a splash of Evian.

"To you," he said and slid one glass across the counter to Sean. "The best of a bad bunch."

"You're very gracious," Sean said touching his glass to Marty's.

"What can I say? My best quality."

They drank the first glass in silence, then Marty refilled them.

"Christ," he said, pointing out the window. "They're all getting fat."

Sean nodded.

"I mean, shit. They're starting to look like their parents. Fat, boring and pathetic."

"Like me."

"Nah, you're just lazy."

"I like to think of it as indecisive."

"Lazy. Indecisive," Marty said. "What's the fucking difference?"

"I guess I'm still trying to figure that one out."

Marty looked at the floor and ran his hand gently through his hair.

"You know what you need, Sean?" Marty said his voice becoming parental. "A change, that's what. A shock to get you moving again. You could start by eighty-sixing that fuck-up job of yours. I mean, what is it, five, six years you've been at that joint?"

"Seven."

"Seven. Shit! That place is like the Black Hole of fucking Calcutta, man. And you fell into it seven years ago. What the hell are you waiting on tables for, anyway? You're a goddam university graduate."

Sean shrugged his shoulders. "I'm doing okay."

"Yeah, right. Minimum wage plus tips."

Sean looked down at himself in Marty's clothes.

"You know what you should do, don't you?" Marty said, pausing only long enough for Sean to purse his lips and shrug. "You should come work with me. I've told you before Shelley's old man can make room for you."

Sean tried to stifle the laugh but doing so only made it sound more derisive, and he could see the twinge of hurt around Marty's eyes. The offer had been made more times than Sean could remember. He almost looked forward to it. If only because it gave him the rare opportunity of holding the high hand.

"Yeah, yeah, I know," Marty said and sipped at his drink. "You're no real estate agent. But I don't know why you couldn't be. It's a piece of cake."

"No," Sean said, shaking his head. "A kind offer, but no."

"Well," Marty sighed, "there's always the restaurant business. I mean, you gotta know it back to front and upside fucking down by now. You should think about opening your own place."

"On minimum wage plus tips?"

Marty cleared his throat and looked into his glass. "Shelley and I got plenty of money," he said.

Sean ran his hand across the soft fabric that stretched over his belly. "How about we pretend you didn't say that."

"Come on, Sean."

Sean moved to the window. Those outside carried on as before. They did look like parents, he thought, puffy and comfortable, if not quite happy.

"It's not like I'd be your boss or anything."

"Marty," Sean said, his voice grown cold. "Just forget it, okay."

"Yeah, you're right. Look, I'm sorry I mentioned it. Really, man." Marty drained his glass. "What do you say we check out the fireworks."

Sean finished another three whiskies while Marty sorted through his Box of Combustible Wonders, choosing what he assured Sean were the loudest, brightest fireworks money could buy. Then Sean helped him carry the lot down to the canoe. Marty had decided that this year he was going to conduct his show from the raft, counting on the setting to add that much more clout to his demonstration.

Sean stood on the shore and watched Marty paddle through the twilight toward the raft. He lit a cigarette and closed his eyes, feeling the nicotine mix with the whisky in his head. No one else up for the weekend smoked. At least not anymore. They'd sworn off the habit, telling him he should do the same. Most had replaced it with new, more body-friendly dependencies. It was jogging for some. Others ran toward aerobics or tai-chi, or fat-free diets with beta-carotene chasers. Any form of self-flagellation that might purge their bodies of the ignorance of youth. Still, Sean knew his banishment wouldn't last. And sooner rather than later, they would search him out with innocent grins on their faces, to ask sheepishly if they could have just *one* cigarette. But until then, he was determined to enjoy his exile.

He turned around and looked back at the cottage. Shelley was making her way down the lawn toward him. Even in the greying light her skin was radiant. The sun, so cruel to some, always left her looking healthy.

"Hey there," she said pushing strands of loose blonde hair away from her forehead. "You got one of those for me?"

Sean fumbled in his front pocket for his cigarettes.

"What about Marty?" he asked handing her the pack.

"What he doesn't know won't hurt him."

Sean flicked open his Zippo and lit her cigarette. Shelley drew deeply and the ember flared with neon-brightness then faded.

"My God," she sighed, "that's nice."

"You never really quit, did you?" Sean said.

"Depends on what you mean by quit," Shelley answered taking another drag.

"It usually means stop."

"Well, I only smoke when I'm with you."

"That's close enough, I guess," Sean said. He took a sip from the glass of whisky and watched as Shelley slipped off her sandals and dipped her feet in the water. "So," he said, "who was the redhead you were talking to earlier?"

"That was, if you can believe it, the new soon-to-be Mrs. Pat Michaud."

"Really," Sean said. "I wonder what happened to the old soon-to-be."

"I'm sure Pat doesn't," Shelley said looking back toward the patio with narrowed eyes. "But we don't care about him, do we? How about you? How's what's her name?"

"Gone the way of the dodo, I'm afraid."

"What a charming way to put it," Shelley said and blew smoke toward him.

"Bad joke," Sean said. He could feel a flush of embarrassment creep into his face and he hoped that the light had faded enough that Shelley wouldn't notice.

"So what happened?" she asked.

"Whatever usually happens," Sean shrugged. "It just didn't work out."

"That's too bad. I liked her. You two made a good couple."

"I guess we did for a while but ... I don't know. It just wasn't right."

"Well, Sean," Shelley said, "you can't always expect things to be perfect."

"No, maybe not."

They were quiet for a moment, the only sound that of Sean shifting his feet on the loose stones of the beach. He dug a hole with his toe, then watched it fill in with dark water rising from below. When he looked up, Shelley was watching him.

"Marty had a talk with me," he said.

"Uh-huh."

"Seems he doesn't think much of what I'm doing with myself, either."

"I've never said that, Sean," Shelley said. "Don't put words in my mouth." She glanced out toward the raft. "What did he have to say?"

"Just a little proposition."

"The restaurant thing?"

"You knew about it?"

"Sure," she said absently, letting the smoke curl around her face. "He's been going on about it for almost a year now."

Sean thought about this for a moment. It bothered him that she had known about it, that she and Marty talked about him when he wasn't there.

"So?" he said.

Shelley wrapped her arms around herself, as if she'd been taken with a sudden chill. "I think you should do whatever you want, Sean," she said in a soft, serious voice. "I think you should take what Marty says for what it's worth."

He tried to study her expression in the failing light, but could find nothing revealing in it.

"And what is it worth?" he asked.

Shelley shrugged and threw the butt of her cigarette into the water.

The collected souls oohed and aahed at the screeches and screams that bounced from lake to cottage back to lake again. Their eyes shimmered in the rainbow bursts that showered burning gems onto the surface of the water. And every break in the noise and dazzle was greeted by a lonely satisfied laugh that floated to shore from the raft. Sean stood close to Shelley, his face turned up at the night sky. He could smell the perfume she'd rubbed into the skin of her neck. It mingled with the sulfur smoke of the spent fireworks, creating a deep musky scent that drew him nearer to her. The back of his hand brushed against her thigh as he raised his glass to his lips. Out of the corner of his eye he saw her turn toward him, then look away again. The final burst cracked like a cannon and shot glowing shards through the blackness. Then silence. Marty's voice disturbed the peace.

"Sean, if you drank all my whisky I'll fucking drown you."

People laughed.

"I wish he wouldn't swear so much," Shelley said quietly.

"Part of the show," Sean replied then finished his drink. "I'd better go help him in."

After the fireworks, the games commenced. What would have been Bullshit, Fuzzy Duck and Asshole a few years earlier became Gin Rummy and Trivial Pursuit. Some eschewed games altogether, opting instead for drunken reminiscing. Sean and Marty made for the cover of the kitchen, intent on finishing the whisky undisturbed.

Sean could feel the booze catching up with him. The kitchen floor began to feel like the deck of a ship, rolling gently under his feet.

"Hiding behind your bottle again," Shelley said when she found them draped over the bentwood chairs almost an hour later. Marty raised his sagging head and squinted at her. "Looks like you're running out of gas," she said.

"That's where you're wrong, baby." Marty lifted his glass. "I got plenty of fucking gas left in me."

"Watch your language, okay."

"Hey, that's why you love me" Marty slurred. "Or should I say, *fucking* love me?"

Sean leaned back in the chair and poured another finger of whisky into his glass as Marty rose unsteadily and clumsily wrapped his arms around Shelley's waist. He pulled her close and buried his face in her cleavage. Shelley pushed him away.

"Don't even try it." she said.

"Come *on*, sweetie," Marty said and started to run his hand up the back of Shelley's shorts.

"I said, that's enough!" The force of her voice seemed to surprise even her. Its effect on Marty was sobering, straightening his drunken slouch.

"Christ, Shelley. Lighten up," he said, without the trace of a slur.

"You've had too much to drink," Shelley said flatly.

"Maybe you haven't had enough."

"Jesus, I wish you would grow up, Marty." Shelley slipped a cigarette from Sean's pack lying on the table. She stared at Marty as she lit it. "And in case you haven't noticed, the living room is full of your inebriated friends."

"Right," Marty said, and waved her smoke from his face as he passed.

Sean felt it difficult to look at Shelley once Marty'd left the kitchen. His mind was muddled. All he could think about was the bareness of her leg when he'd brushed his hand against it. He stood up and set his glass on the table, then reached for the whisky again. He could feel his perception fail. The bottom of the bottle clipped his tumbler and sent it shattering to the floor. He stooped quickly and again misjudged the depth. The shard sank numbly into his finger. Even as the blood started to flow he could feel no pain.

"Shit," he mumbled.

"Christ, Sean," Shelley said. "Let me see that."

"It's nothing."

"Give me your hand."

Shelley carefully pulled the glass from his finger then rinsed the cut under the faucet. Her hair slipped in front of her eyes and she tried to blow it away. With his free hand, Sean gently pulled the stray lock away from her face and tucked it behind her ear. She stopped what she was doing and looked at him. He reached out and touched her hair again.

"Sean?"

"Yes."

He tipped his head toward hers. He felt the guilt rush like bile into his throat, but he swallowed it and continued forward. Then he felt the pain.

"Oh fuck!"

Sean saw the skin of his finger flush under Shelley's pressure. The blood fell in heavy drops onto the stainless steel of the sink.

"My God," she said. "I'm sorry, Sean. I didn't mean"

"No, no. Don't worry."

"Here, let me fix it."

"Forget it. It's fine, really."

"I'll get you a Band-Aid."

"Forget it. It's all right." He looked quickly around the kitchen. "I gotta get some air."

Sean slipped into the living room. An eruption of laughter stopped him at the patio doors. He turned to see Marty doubled over in the Barcalounger, Pat Michaud giggling beside him. A pyramid of beer bottles had crashed to the floor in front of them. Sitting on the sofa, the redheaded new soon-to-be Mrs. Michaud had drifted into unconsciousness.

Outside, Sean stuck his finger in his mouth and sucked the cut like a snake bite. The faint rustiness of the blood on his tongue tightened his stomach. He spat the flooding saliva onto the ground in the hope of warding off nausea. It passed slowly and once it had, he sat down on the grass and lit a cigarette. He stayed in the dark just beyond the patio, not wanting anyone inside to see him. The butane from his lighter flowed through the filter of his cigarette and erased the blood from his palate. The laughter that flooded through the glass doors reverberated between his ears; from one to the other and back again, merging with the next bout that drifted out. Again he wanted to throw up. The muscles in his abdomen danced an isometric jig. Then he heard her voice behind him.

"Sean? Sean? Are you okay?"

He felt Shelley's hand caressing his back.

"How you doing there?"

He couldn't make out her face in the dark. "I'm very drunk," he said.

"I think everybody is."

They were quiet for a moment.

"What's going on in there?"

"Well," Shelley said and sat down beside him. "Pretty much everyone's stumbling through the golden oldies, and Pat and his fiancée are fighting in the back bedroom."

"Same old same old," Sean said.

"Yeah."

Sean let his head sink toward his chest. It seemed to him as if the world was moving in slo-mo, advancing shakily frame by frame. His words felt thick and snail-like on his tongue; they emerged with a sluggishness that could not be forced. Shelley's sounded the same to his ears.

"I'm sorry," Sean said. "I'm sorry about what I did in there."

"It's okay."

"No, really."

"Sean, it's all right."

The noise coming from inside sounded hollow and far away. The drunken laughter still poured through the window, but now the glass seemed much thicker. Sean looked at his cigarette. The dew from the grass had smothered the ember. And the stinging in his finger had subsided. He took a deep breath.

"I'm still in love with you," he said.

"I know."

Shelley rubbed a warm spot between his shoulders.

"Do you want to go back inside?" she asked.

"No."

"Do you want to stay here?"

"No." He leaned his head against her shoulder and felt her breath warm against his brow. "Let's go for a walk."

The foulness of the bog hit him with full force. Its reek like a taste. What were the others doing, he wondered: sleeping, puking, fucking drunkenly in one of the back bedrooms. Did anyone even realize they were gone? He looked down. The water was a black stain creeping up over his knees. Marty's shorts would be ruined.

He knew it was a bad idea to come into the woods. But they'd kept on, moving deeper into the forest, until nothing looked familiar. The grey light of the moon, the tiny voices everywhere, the alcohol in his veins, all commingled to make a stew of his senses. Fear brushed over him like feathers, coldly tickling his skin. His balance deserted him. Things began to slip.

The swamp steadied him. The swamp brought order to the whirligig of his mind. It was right where it should be. And beyond the swamp, the hill. It rose up, just as it always had, from the far shore and on through the trees. All they had to do was wade through, climb the hill and hop the fence and they would be home. He told her this as he bent down to retie his shoes.

And she followed. Pulled her laces tight through the eyeholes of tattered desert boots and stepped into the stinking water. The sound of her feet squelching in the mud joined his own.

He'd come this way a thousand times. Home from school. Home. The bottom started to give way. Home. He remembered the fireworks. His blood froze and shattered in his veins. He looked at the inky woods that stretched skyward from the water's edge and disappeared into the darkness. He was not where he'd thought.

There was no sound now except the mud. A filthy mouth opening and closing around their feet.

I don't think this is the right way, he heard her say. And knew she was right. Just a little further, he wanted to tell, but the words caught in his throat.

WINDOWS

"What I'm thinking is a double-hung laid on its edge with a picture across the top. Get a better view that way."

Carol looked but couldn't see. She made a face.

"I'd just cut it down about a foot...here—" The contractor took the pencil from behind his ear. He scratched his thought on the back of Carol's telephone bill. "See?" he said, holding it up to the window.

"Yes," Carol said. "That looks fine."

"Now," he went on, "for the bedroom you'll want a tilt and turn. Something that you can open wide in case you need to get out in a hurry."

Carol wasn't listening. She was thinking. About the windows and the way they looked: quaint, countrified; how when the sun came through them it was quartered by the wooden trim that sectioned the glass; how the panes were thicker at the bottom than the top because glass is liquid and always in motion. How they once reminded Bill of a New England farmhouse, somewhere in Vermont, though he had never been there.

She had hit a child after Bill left. The boy was fifteen years old, his hair cut close to his scalp, Doc Martens to mid-calf, slogans painted on the back of his jean jacket. The sound of her open palm on his face was like wet on wet. The boy cried, there beside her desk, in front of the entire class. Carol tried to feel bad, to feel ashamed, but couldn't. She wanted to hit him again.

That was four weeks ago. The principal had been frantic, anxious about a lawsuit. He had sent her home, told her to take as long as she needed. A few days later he'd called to say things had been smoothed over. "A knife," he said. "Found it during a random locker search." But she wasn't to come back, not yet. He made reference to an environment of accusation and said, "We'll put it down as stress leave. No one will be bothered about that."

Carol was bothered about it. She felt foolish and angry. The madwoman in the attic, unable to master her emotions; an hysteric. There would be talk in the teachers' lounge, both during her absence and after. Maybe she wouldn't return. She could probably find another school. At thirty-seven another vocation would be more difficult. She realized, though it didn't seem possible, that when it came to certain things, she was old. Music and movies had left her behind. And her education, a commodity fifteen years ago, had lost its currency. Her knowledge was vinyl.

The contractor's name was Peter. He was wide through the shoulders with thick meaty hands. The belly that pushed over his jeans made no apology. And there was a haziness about him, as if he had been blown over with plaster dust. He was slow to smile. Before he even looked at the windows he asked if he could plant a sign on the lawn. Advertising, he called it. He had no doubt he would procure the job. Nor had Carol. She found his number in the yellow pages and called no others.

Bill would have been furious, doubly so. To replace the windows was bad enough. They were the only thing that gave the house character, that separated it from all the other pre-war cottages on their tree-shaded block; he loved them, with their original sashes and mullions and jambs and sills. But more galling would be the fact that she hadn't price-compared, hadn't rooted out a deal. She'd not even asked for an estimate.

Carol followed Peter into the bedroom. She stood to the side while he stretched his tape measure. He noted length, width and depth. Then held his hand a few inches from the glass.

"Got a draft here," he said.

The room had always been cold. Bill liked it that way, said it made him feel refreshed. Carol would get out extra blankets.

"Do you get midges?" Peter asked.

"Sorry?"

"Midges. Little flies. They buzz around the lights at night. Dead by morning."

"Yes," Carol said. "Quite a lot in the summer."

"I'll bet," he said, rattling the glass. "They come in around the frame. Wood's shrunk. Not to worry, we'll seal it up like a vault." He made a pencil mark on the sill. "The tilt and turn will swing all the way back, like a door. Easy to clean."

Carol realized as Peter stood there that no other man aside from Bill had ever been in that room with her. She imagined the contractor in his undershorts, stretching himself and scratching, sifting through the bureau for fresh clothes. He would have dark hair on his chest and back, curled tight like a scouring pad. His smell would be musky. For Carol this was the intimacy of a bedroom. The thought was not unpleasant, but neither was it agreeable. It was simply a thought.

Bill had a stale odour. Old cloth, parchment. He wore briefs, parted his hair on the side with a stiff brush, hung his suit jackets according to fabric, separated his loose change. In bed his body was sharp angles, but Carol had learned how to negotiate its terrain safely, to mold herself to his edges. She had not slept in their bed since he left. The sofa was her berth now, lying awake late into the night, until the television showed colour bars.

"Is that it then?" she asked.

"For measuring, sure," Peter said. "Just have to go over the numbers."

"I'll make coffee."

He sat opposite her at the kitchen table, his head down, the order form before him. Like Bill working at his crossword puzzle, silent, his coffee cooling at his elbow, waiting to be swallowed in a single gulp before he left for work. She lifted her cup to her lips and quietly sipped. She watched him furrow his brow, cross out a figure and rewrite it. Then he pushed the form toward her.

"I've got you down for seven double-hungs, three pictures and the tilt and turn. The sizes are here." Peter ran his thick finger down a column of measurements. "And we've gone for Low E Argon glass with thermal edging." He smiled. "That'll take care of your draft."

Carol lifted the paper. The penmanship was careless. A mixture of the written and the printed that verged on illegible. Words and numbers were buried under chaotic swirls of ink. Had he been her student, his grade would have suffered.

"If you want," Peter said, "you can have your husband look it over."

"I don't have a husband."

Carol followed his gaze. The band on her finger. She had not realized it until then. There was no feeling of it against her skin. No more than a bump on her flesh.

"He's gone," she said.

"I'm very sorry."

She decided not to correct his assumption, rather accepted the sympathy.

"I can give you a rebate," he said. Carol noted a catch in his voice. "Since we're doing the entire house I can offer ten percent."

"That would be very nice," she said and smiled how she thought a widow might. "When will you start?"

"Sign at the bottom and I'll file the work order. A week Tuesday I'd say."

Carol took up his pen. The end was chewed. The nervous habit of so many adolescents. She could not imagine this large man fidgety.

"I wonder," she said, sliding the document back across the table, "if you might be able to start with the bedroom?"

"That's what you like." He folded the paper in thirds and slipped it into his breast pocket.

"Yes." Carol stood up. "The bedroom, I think."

THE HAPPY PILGRIM

The sun crept over the Pyrenees. Daniel Green could not see it; he couldn't even see the mountains. He knew it was there, though, inching its way above the rock, because he was able to observe the men moving in the yard below his window. When they had begun to unload the *camionnette* they were concealed by darkness. Now they worked under a veil of grey, like crabs scuttling along the bottom of a murky pool. Daniel lit a cigarette, though he knew it would not ease the pain in his head, an ache that burrowed like a chigger into his temples. Below him, sacks of liver, tongue, intestines and blood were stacked against the stone wall. He had stopped eating meat shortly after he arrived. Daniel never told this to the *charcutier*, nor the *charcutier's* wife, who offered him gifts of paté and sweetbread. He accepted these *viandes* with a smile, but later passed them on to Victor or someone at the agency. It would have been rude to refuse them; the old man and his wife laboured so, to transform the offal into delicacies.

After he'd finished his cigarette, and the *camionnette* had backed out of the yard, Daniel lifted his tie, already knotted, from the bedpost and slipped it over his head. Then he took up his watch from the night table. It was gold-plated with a linked band, a gift from his parents. They'd given it to him the night he left, at the restaurant where they'd taken him for his farewell dinner.

Before sliding it onto his wrist, he reread the inscription on its back: "Go With God, Mother & Father." There had been a time when he'd considered the priesthood. His father drove him to St. Basil's, where Daniel asked questions about the seminary. He was fifteen. By the time he was sixteen, he wanted to be a veterinarian. He no longer entertained thoughts of either.

The grey outside his window turned dun. The bells would start soon, ringing out the hour with an Ave Maria from high in the tower of the Basilica. The hymn had lost its meaning for Daniel; it was no more than an annoyance to him now. One the eager sextons would not permit him to block out. He picked up his satchel and checked to make sure his clipboard and itinerary were inside, then moved to the door. On the small ledge beside the coat rack were the last two letters his parents had sent him. Daniel ran his fingers across his mother's spidery script. She would have addressed the envelopes and affixed their stamps after returning from early mass at St. Michael's; she'd have lit a candle and offered a prayer for his well-being. Daniel left the letters unopened.

Sister Mary Bernard struggled to breathe under the weight of her lungs. The stain of consumption made the simple act of taking in air almost unbearable. And the blood brought forth by her coughing soiled her palate as much as it did the rag she used to wipe it away. Anklyosis swelled her knees to twice their normal size, refusing to allow the joints to move. If she remained still, the pain was like a stagnant pool, festering but calm.

They would come soon, to pray over her and bathe her with cold cloths. Her suffering, she knew, was heaven sent. A test and testimony of her faith. The glory of the next life would most definitely be hers, but why must it take so long to come? Her cell was cold and draughty. The moisture froze on the grey stones of the floor and walls. A thin blanket covered her body. In the mattress beneath her, she could feel the bedbugs crawl.

When they came, they would turn her on her side and remove the rough linen sheet she lay upon. It would be stained with blood and suppuration, and when they folded it, they would fold with it strips of her sodden flesh. Then they would cleanse the sores that carpeted her back. The coolness would offer relief, but only temporarily. Soon the torrent of pain would return.

To escape these afflictions, Sister Mary Bernard thought of her childhood. She had never been healthy, but the asthma that plagued her as a young girl seemed salubrious by comparison. Shivering in her damp cell, she would follow the winding mountain road once again, as it tracked its way through St. Savin, with its crumbling monastery, and onto the spa at Cauterets. She travelled there to take the cure, just as Julius Caesar had centuries before. If she had only been educated then, she could have written of the wonders she saw. Cauterets was a place of elegance, so foreign to her: the Esplanade des Oeufs with its lavish arcades and daunting casino, the resplendent avenues and the mountain current that bisected the town, the church with its modest statue of the Virgin, where she knelt to pray, though for what she could no longer recall. But she had been an ignorant girl, versed in nothing, and had to commit these spectacles to memory. And it was this memory that she now held suspect, knowing that time must embellish.

The heat of the day arrived early, like an eager and unwanted dinner guest. Daniel wished he had brought along his wide-brimmed cotton sun hat, or at least his handkerchief. But he had neither and perspiration bubbled on his brow and ran like teardrops into his eyes. The heat also played havoc with his breakfast, two rich pastries and three café crèmes that sat like stones in the pit of his belly. The swelter seemed to add to their weight. He still had the slightest twinge of a headache and he thought he could taste Pernod in the film of sweat that glazed his top lip. The smell of the creosote-soaked railway ties did not help matters. Daniel could feel his stomach begin to turn.

Further down the busy platform he could see the group organizers, two men whose pale skin was clearly unaccustomed to the hard sun. Daniel had met them at the hotel the previous afternoon. They'd flown into Tarbes a day ahead of their charges, ostensibly to make certain the arrangements had been taken care of, though Daniel expected their early arrival had more to do with escaping the arduous rail journey from London. As he started toward them the Tannoy came to life: two loud clicks, a low moan, then the hollow notes of a pipe organ. When the choir started in, their voices sounded metallic through the loudspeakers. The train would be passing the Grotto on the opposite side of the Gave de Pau. If he turned, Daniel would be able to see the engine. He did not turn. He put a smile on his face and greeted the two men.

"Bloody hot," the short, pudgy one said, his cheeks crimson.

"Yes, Mr. Philbert," Daniel replied. "The weather here can be deceiving. You'd expect it to be cooler in the mountains, but you must remember we are quite far south."

"I'd wager they're near cooked by now," the other

chuckled, pointing to the train as it pulled alongside the platform.

When Daniel arrived, he too had come by train. But there'd been no one to meet him at the station. He disembarked, laden with an enormous backpack, onto an empty platform. And he couldn't find anyone willing to extend the courtesy of patience when he stumbled with his French. The handwritten directions that had been included with his employment contract did not jibe with the map in his guidebook. The city stood before him like a maze, its narrow streets folding back on themselves; completely foreign to the compass-point civil engineering of Toronto.

He found the offices of Holy Days Holidays Travel Agency on the second floor of an austere granite-stone townhouse on the Avenue du Paradis. The receptionist, a tall, thin woman with a bruised complexion who introduced herself, in stilted English, as Madame Oiseau, offered him a seat in the anteroom. Daniel waited there for over an hour, struggling to stay awake. Whenever his head dipped toward his chest, a chirp from Madame Oiseau straightened it again. And when she found that Daniel would no longer obey her interruptions, she got to her feet.

"Now, Monsieur Green," she said. "Now you may go in." She held the door open.

"Then the king commanded," a thick Irish brogue thundered from within, "and they brought Daniel and cast him into the den of lions." Oliver Conmee, manager of the Lourdes office of Holy Days Holidays Travel Agency was seated behind a wide mahogany desk that pushed up against his massive belly. His face was florid and a great drooping moustache hid completely the grin underneath. He did not get up to greet Daniel. Instead, he motioned to a chair, "Sit, sit."

The room smelled of stale pipe tobacco. Daniel

fidgeted in the over-stuffed chair. The seat beneath him felt as if it were designed to upset his balance rather than welcome his weight. Conmee, on the other hand, seemed overly concerned with Daniel's comfort, wanting to know if he'd found a place to live yet.

"There are any number of homes on the road to Tarbes," Conmee said, stroking his moustache, "that take in boarders. But I wouldn't recommend them. Nasty little places, they are. Rooms so small you can't turn round without hitting a wall." However, he knew of a flat that was available. It was situated above a *charcuterie* on Rue de la Grotte, near the Poor Clares Convent. "It's quite cheap," Conmee said, "I could even arrange to have the rent taken straight from your wage packet."

It was almost as an afterthought that Conmee explained the duties of the job. "You will be," Oliver Conmee said, as he stuffed his ebony pipe, "the *liaison des pèlerin*. It's a fancy title, I'll warrant, but they like fancy in Lourdes. Essentially you are in charge of our 'budget tours'. Meet them at the rail station, get them settled at the hotel, iron out any problems, answer any questions. And at the end of their trip, you make certain they all make it back to the train. That's important, that is. It's all in here." Conmee slid a thick manila envelope across his desk. He lit his pipe and blew a grey cloud toward Daniel. "Don't worry about getting them to the Grotto, or the baths, or the Basilica. That's their pilgrimage organizer's job. And they've got their own doctors and *brancardiers* to attend to the sick. Must remember, our concern isn't the spiritual, it's the practical. If you have any questions, don't hesitate to ask Madame Oiseau." And that was it.

When she was thirteen, Sister Mary Bernard was sent by her parents to Bartes. There she lived with her former foster-mother, the woman who had suckled her when her own mother's illness stole her milk. It was a year of famine; although, since her father had lost his position at the mill, most every year had been one of famine. And the *cachot* where her family lived — taken after they were turned out of their own home — was a wretched place. Even the police had abandoned it, finding it unfit to house criminals. Six of them lived there, sharing the meagre space with the rats and filth, always aware of their deprivation. Day by day, the melancholia that devoured her father's soul fed on the very air of the *cachot*, consuming its light. Candles burned in every corner of the room, but their flames could not prick the darkness. The only spark of any intensity was that of her mother's fury. It blazed with fingernails and open palms, kindled by circumstance. Bartes was her release. It was clean air, warm food and a bed she did not have to share with three.

Sister Mary Bernard thought of the small flock she had tended. The sheep grazed on the edge of the village. Grubby animals, their wool matted and fouled by their own grime, but she did not care, they obeyed her cane and ate grasses from her hand. The wind that blew over the mountains was pure. Her lungs did not reject it. There was a child, too. She watched over him as if he were her own. And dreamt of the time when she might become a mother herself.

When word came from her father that she was to return, she wept, then begged to be allowed to stay. No one listened. She may as well have asked the mountains to move. From that moment onward, she could only ever think of her seven months of happiness in Bartes as a cruel joke.

The pilgrims were singing when they got off the train, and they were singing when they got on the coach. There were a few grumblers who complained about the stale sandwiches and the rudeness of the porters at Bordeaux. For the most part, though, the group was affable. They were English pilgrims and Daniel liked the English, found them jovial. Unlike the Irish, who held to a strict piety; or the Welsh, who could be tight-lipped and cool, or so blithe as to make the English appear stoic; in this way, the Welsh were very much like the native Lourdais. In this new group, however, there was a gentleman from Birmingham, whose accent struggled for the Home Counties, who demanded to know why they were being met by an American.

"Actually, sir," Daniel said, "I'm Canadian. From Toronto."

"Why you people insist on making the distinction is beyond me," the man said. "I should expect a Briton to greet a British pilgrimage." Then he turned and boarded the coach.

The singing diminished as the coach inched through the already clogged streets of the High Town. Like tourists on a site-seeing trip, the pilgrims crowded the windows. The object of their curiosity, however, was not the ancient architecture of the city, but the seemingly endless array of vulgar boutiques that lined the street. The pavements were cluttered with displays: racks bearing plastic Virgins with eyes that blinked red and green, tables strewn with Virgins with bobbing heads, Virgins dressed in flags of many nations, decanter Virgins, telephone Virgins, desk-lamp Virgins and Virgins that recited prayers at the pull of a cord. This was the domain of the *commerçants*. And while the pilgrims looked upon this spectacle with a shade of disgust on their faces, Daniel knew that, beneath this disapproval, they were trying to decide which of the knick-knacks they would take home with them.

There had been none of this when Daniel arrived. But with the opening of the pilgrimage season the *commerçants* had sprung up overnight, like toadstools pushing through the loamy soil of a fine garden. The quaint provincial streets transmogrified into a casbah before his eyes, the merchants like hawkers shouting their wares. *They've made a sideshow of Lourdes*, Daniel wrote to his parents. *The commerçants have corrupted it with their gaudy baubles and shimmering trinkets. It looks like Niagara Falls. I am reminded of the money-changers in the temple.*

During his first weeks in the city, Daniel had thoughts of tearing down the stalls, of overturning the tables and dashing the gimcracks against the paving stones. He'd even wondered about blacking out the windows of the coaches to shield the pilgrims from corruption, until he realized that it was the souvenir traders almost as much as the Grotto that brought the travellers to Lourdes.

I feel soiled, he said in another letter, *complicit.* And when one of these merchants, a brick-like man with dark eyes and scruffy cheeks, took hold of his arm and pressed a damp wad of francs into his palm, Daniel knew what it meant, and it was all he could do to keep from striking him.

"*Je ne veux ça pas*," he blurted, the words tangling on his tongue. "*Tu est dégoutant.*"

The man laughed at him, but did not release his arm. Rather, he squeezed harder until Daniel could feel a tingling in his elbow. It was as if his bones were being compressed in a vice. Then the man let go and, with a smile still on his face, spoke in a voice so soft it belied his largeness.

"*Ton français est affreux.* You should stick to English."

The sound of his own language on the man's lips confused Daniel. It was not that the Lourdais did not speak English — many did. It was the fluidity with which he spoke it, all but untouched by the heavy hand of the local patois.

"Take your money," Daniel said, pushing the roll of bills into the man's chest.

"You would like pigeons, maybe? I can bring you pigeons. Or perhaps you wish to hunt them yourself?"

"Nothing," Daniel hissed. "I want nothing."

"I have been watching you," the man said, returning the francs to his pocket. "I believe you have a good heart. But here." He tapped a finger against his forehead. "Here you are *insuffisant*."

"I beg your pardon."

"To live in Lourdes," the merchant continued, as if Daniel hadn't spoken, "is like to live in Paris. Much more than you can afford. This I know."

Daniel turned to walk away, but the big Frenchman's hand spun him on his heels.

"One has to live, *monsieur*. You need me, I need you. Your disgust is irrelevant. What I propose is business only." He threw an arm around Daniel's shoulder and pulled him close; then he patted Daniel's belly with his free hand. "Think about it," he said. "Tonight. When you are eating your stale baguette."

Daniel almost fell to the ground when the man let him go.

"I should introduce myself," the *commerçant* added. "I am Victor Bousquiere."

It was true, the *cachot* was insufferable. But when Sister Mary Bernard was taken from it at the age of fifteen, she missed it terribly. Her health, always poor, had again deteriorated. Father Peyramale, concerned by this turn, facilitated her move to the Hospice of the Sisters of Nevers. Lying there, in her own bed, separated from the other invalids on the ward, she longed for the crowded slumber she shared with her younger sisters; she missed the warmth of their bodies, a comfort no amount of blankets could offer her. On days when she felt well enough, she was permitted by the nuns to visit her family. On these occasions, she was accompanied by one of the Sisters, who held her arm during the short journey down the hill and across the bridge spanning the Lapacca Torrent. Her guardian would also intercept the apprach of strangers.

She loved these times she spent with her brother and sisters. It allowed her the chance to be a child again and she played with a vigour heightened by her absence. The moment she entered the *cachot*, it was as if she and her siblings had never been apart, as if nothing had changed. This was not so with her parents. They looked upon her differently and spoke in hushed tones. Her mother kept her eyes averted; her hands remained folded in her lap. Her father, though he seemed to want to take her into his arms, would only touch her lightly on the shoulder. They did not ask when she was to return home.

Although he had expected as much, Daniel had held out hope that it wouldn't happen. On first sight, the pilgrims were pleased with La Maison d'Immaculado Concepciou. Built at the turn of the century on the left bank of the Gave de Pau, it exuded Parisian quality. French windows along the east-side of the hotel offered a superb view of the old quarter across the river. The bar terrace itself reached to the water's edge and it had the look and feel of a Montparnasse café. It was here, seated at an umbrellaed table, sipping warm mineral water, that Daniel awaited the inevitable. He was not halfway through the bottle when Mr. Philbert, his collar stained with sweat, huffed and puffed his way between the tightly set tables. His bulk, when it landed in the chair, sent a shiver through the wrought iron table.

"Seems we've run into a few problems," he gasped. "More than a few, actually."

"Really?" Daniel sighed. He'd grown tired of this game. He knew the litany of complaints even before Mr. Philbert wheezed them out: backed-up commodes, leaking faucets, broken bedsteads, malfunctioning locks, misassigned rooms. But he let the man talk anyway. He wanted time to finish his drink before he began the ritualistic parrying with the hotelier. In the end, the most adamant complainants would be satisfied and the rest would be led to believe that they were making virtuous sacrifices.

When Daniel had told Victor Bousquiere of this repetitive scenario, the big Frenchman laughed until his entire body shook like jelly. They were at the Lourdais café they'd taken to frequenting. Victor never once mentioned his capitulation, for which Daniel was grateful. To lighten his embarrassment, Daniel had delivered to Victor a stale baguette with his answer. The Frenchman, giggling, had kissed him full on the lips. In the café, after he'd stopped laughing, Victor put his hand on Daniel's shoulder and asked him, in the same patient voice as when they'd first met, who did he think these hoteliers were?

"I will tell you," Victor said. "These are the same people who slapped the face of a saint. The same ones who spat on her in the street for bringing shame on this pleasant village. Even the blessed Peyramale allowed the police to interrogate her like a common criminal. A young girl she was and they threaten her with prison. It did not matter that she already lived in a dungeon.

They would lock her up anyway. For inciting public disorder." Victor looked over his shoulder and down Boulevard de la Grotte and laughed again. "Public disorder, indeed."

"But that was over a century ago, Victor."

"Who is it, Daniel, that prospers?" Victor asked, his tone solemn, his lips unsmiling. "Is it you? Is it me? *La famille* Soubirous, maybe? They ended up selling bibelots like myself. No. I will tell you who it is that prospers. It is the fat lady with the fur collar who slaps a little girl. And she still lives, this fat lady, in the hotelier of La Maison d'Immacculado Concepciou and all the others."

She joined the Sisters of the Order of Nevers because they did not pursue her. For six years she lived in their Hospice, her health and needs attended to, her education supplied, and they never pressed her into their fold. When the public's hunger for her made it impossible to journey into town, they did not try to enlist her as a novelty. Other orders courted her. The Carmelites and the Sisters of the Cross. But their reasons had more to do with their own status than her vocation. For many, her maladies were determined to be too great a burden. Even the Bernadines had rejected her on this basis. As for the Sisters of Saint Vincent de Paul, she found their headdress almost as constricting as her own poor health.

She made her decision on the morning the statue of the Virgin was dedicated in the Grotto. Father Peyramale had wanted her to attend, but she refused. She could no longer stand being in public. The devotion of strangers, their neediness and desire, struck her as obscene. They laid their prayers at her feet as if she were the holy one. Where once they had looked upon her with derision, now they gazed with the countenance of votaries. And though Father Peyramale had done her many kindnesses, she would not go. She took communion at the Hospice chapel, then told the Superior of her intent.

The Sisters of the Order of Nevers made only the smallest display of her investment: two photographs. In the first, she stood alongside the nuns, her flesh drawn and pallid, as Bernadette Soubirous. In the second, still sickly pale, she wore the habit of the Order of Nevers, and stood amongst her peers as Sister Mary Bernard.

The negotiations were theatrically delicate. Daniel exploded into a furious rant — in English and without profanity, just as Oliver Conmee had directed him. The hotelier played his role, as well, complete with his own indignant tirade *en français*. The tweedy pilgrim from Birmingham, however, was far from satisfied by their dramatics. Having been roomed with a fellow of Portuguese extraction, as he put it, he demanded recompense. This was not part of the script. Daniel knew that the hotelier, no matter how pleased with his performance, would not agree to free up the change in his pocket, let alone refund any payment on a room.

"Please, sir. If you'll just bear with me," Daniel smiled. "Lourdes can be a very complicated place. Sometimes we are required to show a little charity."

"Charity, my good man, has no place here." The man was rigid. His speech a twill of inflections. "I give my alms to the poor, to the needy. Neither this Monsieur Portugal nor the innkeeper seems particularly destitute. Thus, there seems little call for my philanthropy. To put it simply, I have paid for a single room and I expect a single room. If this is impossible, which it does appear to be, then I expect reimbursement." He smiled triumphantly, the corners of his tight little mouth curling ever-so-slightly upward.

Daniel wanted to slap the man's face. A great, open-palmed, full-force smack that would rattle his teeth. But he knew the man to be completely within his rights. For no reason should he expect not to get what he'd paid for. Anywhere else his request would have been accommodated, reparations made and apologies proffered. But this was Lourdes. And in Lourdes both hoteliers and travel agents were complicit in the exploitation of Christian goodwill. Daniel could not say this.

"Let me run back to the office," he said. "See if I can't straighten this out. In the meantime, there's a lovely boutique just across the Old Bridge. It's a reputable shop. The prices are fair and the merchandise quality. I know the owner, he's very dependable."

She cried for days after she joined the Order. Why she wept, Sister Mary Bernard could no longer recall. Was it that she was never to be Bernadette Soubirous again? But that name, that personage, had become a torment to her. Had it been her family, whom she lost to the hysteria? She heard talk of their ventures, surviving on the sale of 'religious' articles: scraps of cloth that had touched her body, cups she had drunk from and cups she had not. Or was it joy? Joy that she had given herself, body and soul, over to the Lord? According to the Superior, this was the reason for her tears. Father Peyramale believed this, too. And although Sister Mary Bernard tried to convince herself the same, the sobs that convulsed her body felt as if they issued from another spring entirely. One of loss, not gain.

When it was decided that she be removed from

Lourdes to the Convent of St. Gilgard in Nevers, she complied without argument.

Oliver Conmee was not happy to see Daniel. He had explained to him before how these matters were to be handled. These were *budget* pilgrims, easy to please. "If you can't guilt them into it, then offer them bloody trappings," Conmee shouted. "Give them a dinner. A bottle of champagne. Vouchers for the Miraculous Miracle Show or the Diorama, I don't care. But never money. You know that."

"It won't work, Mr. Conmee," Daniel shrugged. "He won't budge."

Conmee threw up his arms, then got on the phone to the hotelier of La Maison d'Immaculado Concepciou. Daniel sat in the wing chair opposite him and looked around the office. The carpet was a deep mauve pile and the walls were covered in supple cream paper, the floral design of which was more discernible to the touch than the eye. The ceilings were high and decorated in plaster reliefs: angels offering vines thick with grapes. The mahogany desk was polished to a near glow and two jade-shaded brass lamps stood like sentries at the top corners. File cabinets of the same expensive lumber ran the length of one wall and two French windows that climbed almost to the ceiling gave onto the street. The only unpleasant furnishing in the room was Oliver Conmee. The smoke from his pipe, which appeared to have avoided every other surface in the room, seemed to have soaked into his very flesh. There was a haziness to his corpulence. Daniel did not like Conmee. And sitting there, he recalled what Victor had once said of him: "Ah, yes. I know your round Irishman. I do not think he prays."

Daniel rose from the chair. He felt Conmee's eyes

follow him as he crossed to the window. The street below was crowded with pilgrims. They milled about timidly, not set on any particular direction. Those able-bodied looked guilty in their deportment, stepping shyly out of the paths of the brancardiers who pushed the sick in their rickshaw-like wheelchairs. He could not make out individual faces, but this did not matter. He knew they shared the same look. Not even their devout smiles could hide the underlying truth. They were desperate. Each one had started their journey full of expectation. And Daniel knew that as each minute passed, their hope faded. Each was one among millions. Since St. Bernadette had witnessed the apparitions, there had been fifty-one recognized miracles. Fifty-one. It was like trying to win the lottery. Daniel thought of his mother lighting candles at St. Michael's.

"Settled," Conmee barked, slamming down the phone. "The Limey's got his wish. They're going to move that other fellow in with some Italians down the corridor."

"That should make him happy," Daniel said.

Sister Mary Bernard could feel the pain seep from her body. She felt lighter. And it was no longer so difficult to breathe. It would be soon now, before the Sisters came to bathe her.

They had asked her earlier if she had seen the Lady again. They were certain she would. A vessel, they called her, through which mysteries were revealed. One recounted for her her own story: a peasant girl in rags foraging for sticks and bones, who found instead the Mother of God in the fissure of a stone; an angelic child who clawed through the mud and exposed the healing spring. Sister Mary Bernard smiled at them. She knew the Madonna would not return.

Daniel stood on the Old Bridge and stared into the Gave de Pau. The water below him was soupy. And it would be that much more sullied by the time it wound its way passed the Grotto. A receptacle for the waste of the cottages, restaurants, hotels and hospital that inhabited its banks, the river carried the filth of Lourdes away from the city. Even the water of the miraculous spring found its way into the adulterated tributary, where it commingled with the swill until it reached the Atlantic. Daniel leaned over the railing.

"I hope you are not contemplating a leap." Victor Bousquiere smiled and patted his friend's shoulder. "The fall might not kill you, but I have no doubt the water would. Besides, I would miss you."

Victor produced a small roll of francs.

"It was a very good day for business. Your English pilgrims were quite generous."

Daniel slipped the money into his pocket. He took out a cigarette, then offered one to Victor. They stood quietly and smoked. The bells of the Basilica tolled the hour with yet another Ave Maria. Soon the Domain of the Grotto would be crowded with the evening processions. Dilatory pilgrims throughout the city would now be scrambling to buy candles.

"I almost forgot," Victor said, throwing his cigarette into the Pau. "I have brought you something." He retrieved a bag that he'd set on the ground and took from it a small woodcarving of the Virgin Mary mounted within an antiquarian horseshoe. "This is the last of the line," he said. "I buy them from the mental institution. The patients create them. The doctors say it is very therapeutic. But, unfortunately, they have run out of horseshoes and can make no more. This is the last. I thought you might like to send it to your parents."

"That's very kind of you, Victor," Daniel said, and thought of the unopened letters. "They'll appreciate this very much."

"It is gauche, I know," Victor shrugged. "But that is Lourdes."

Daniel dropped his cigarette over the bridge, then tucked the statuette into his satchel.

"Well, my friend," Victor said, clapping Daniel on the shoulder again. "Enough sight-seeing for today. Let us eat. And later I have arranged for us to meet for drinks with two lovely chambermaids. They are Irish, but devoutly unpious."

Daniel Green shared the big man's laughter as they left the bridge and started toward Rue de la Grotte. The pilgrimage season was not yet half over.

There *had* been one revenant, the morning before, but Sister Mary Bernard told no one. It was a boy, her brother, now a grown man. He knelt on the floor of her cell, picking candle wax from the stones to fill his empty belly, just as he had done in the church of their childhood.